U0025466

永恆的莎士比亞改寫劇本 ❺

李爾王

KING LEAR

William Shakespeare ◆ 著

Emily Hutchinson ◆ 改寫 ｜ 蘇瑞琴 ◆ 譯

MP3

永恆的莎士比亞改寫劇本 ❺
李爾王
KING LEAR

作　　者	William Shakespeare, Emily Hutchinson
翻　　譯	蘇瑞琴
編　　輯	Gina Wang
校　　對	代雲芳
內文排版	劉秋筑
封面設計	林書玉
製程管理	洪巧玲
出 版 者	寂天文化事業股份有限公司
電　　話	+886-(0)2-2365-9739
傳　　真	+886-(0)2-2365-9835
網　　址	www.icosmos.com.tw
讀者服務	onlineservice@icosmos.com.tw
出版日期	2016 年 9 月 初版一刷

郵撥帳號 1998620-0 寂天文化事業股份有限公司
劃撥金額 600（含）元以上者，郵資免費。
訂購金額 600 元以下者，加收 65 元運費。
〔若有破損，請寄回更換，謝謝〕

國家圖書館出版品預行編目 (CIP) 資料

永恆的莎士比亞改寫劇本 . 5：李爾王 / William
Shakespeare, Emily Hutchinson 作；蘇瑞琴譯 . -- 初版 . --
[臺北市]：寂天文化 , 2016.09
面；　公分
ISBN 978-986-318-499-7(平裝附光碟片)
873.43359　　　　　　　　　　　　　105016819

Contents

Background 4
Cast of Characters 5

ACT 1
Scene 1 7
Scene 2 20
Scene 3 25
Scene 4 27
Scene 5 38

ACT 2
Scene 1 41
Scene 2 47
Scene 3 51
Scene 4 52

ACT 3
Scene 1 63
Scene 2 65
Scene 3 68
Scene 4 70
Scene 5 74
Scene 6 75
Scene 7 78

ACT 4
Scene 1 85
Scene 2 88
Scene 3 93
Scene 4 95
Scene 5 97
Scene 6 99
Scene 7 107

ACT 5
Scene 1 113
Scene 2 116
Scene 3 117

中文翻譯 132
Literary Glossary 208

Background 🎧

King Lear, a stubborn and proud old man, decides to divide his kingdom among his three daughters. He'll give the largest share to the one who loves him most. Unable to tell the difference between flattery and sincere love, he banishes his youngest daughter, the honest Cordelia. He divides the kingdom between Goneril and Regan. These two "gilded serpents" stop pretending affection. They work together to strip him of every possession, no longer pretending any affection. Lear slowly goes mad, but in his lowest state he begins to know himself as a human being.

Like Lear, Gloucester is also blind to the evil he has fathered—in his illegitimate son Edmund. He sees the truth only after he has been literally blinded by his enemies and saved from despair and suicide by his son Edgar. Evil does its worst to both Lear and Gloucester—but the positive result of their physical destruction is spiritual renewal.

4

Cast of Characters

LEAR: King of Britain

KING OF FRANCE: one of Cordelia's suitors

GONERIL: Lear's eldest daughter

DUKE OF ALBANY: Goneril's husband

REGAN: Lear's second daughter

DUKE OF CORNWALL: Regan's husband

CORDELIA: Lear's youngest daughter

DUKE OF BURGUNDY: one of Cordelia's suitors

EARL OF KENT: loyal member of Lear's court

EARL OF GLOUCESTER: loyal member of Lear's court

EDGAR: Gloucester's elder son, later disguised as Poor Tom, a ragged beggar

EDMUND: Gloucester's younger, illegitimate son

OSWALD: Goneril's steward

CURAN: Gloucester's servant

OLD MAN: Gloucester's tenant

DOCTOR

FOOL: Lear's jester

KNIGHTS, OFFICERS, MESSENGERS, SOLDIERS, SERVANTS, and **ATTENDANTS**

ACT 1

Summary

本劇開始時,李爾王宮廷的忠臣葛勞塞斯特伯爵向另一位朝臣肯特伯爵介紹他的私生子艾德蒙。正當兩人相談甚歡時號角聲響起,宣布李爾王、國王之女、她們兩位丈夫阿爾邦尼公爵和康沃爾公爵來到現場。出其不意地,李爾王宣布他將把王國分給他的女兒——里根、貢納莉和考狄利婭。當李爾王附加說明他將把最大的國土分給最愛他的女兒,貢納莉和里根便開始花言巧語、阿諛奉承,但考狄利婭卻直接說她對父王的愛「如一般女兒應盡孝道,既不多,亦不少」。李爾認為這段話是對他的侮辱,並將她驅逐出王國。

肯特伯爵反對李爾王如此倉促的決定,李爾王稱他為叛徒,也將他驅逐出境。本來已與考狄利婭訂婚的勃艮第公爵,不願意娶沒有家產可繼承的考狄利婭為妻,而同時在現場的法王利用這個機會,親自向考狄利婭提親。當他和考狄利婭離開時,里根和貢納莉討論國王如此不理性的行為,並開始研商要如何反抗他。

在此期間,妒忌心重的艾德蒙企圖摧毀其兄長艾德加(葛勞塞斯特伯爵的婚生子)的名聲。被驅逐出境的肯特偽裝身分,希望能被李爾雇用為宮廷僕人,以試圖保衛國王的利益。本幕接近尾聲時,李爾的弄臣警告他將陷入險境,因為貢納莉和里根開始展現對她們父王的邪惡企圖。

Scene ❶ 🎧

England. A room of state in King Lear's palace. **Kent**, **Gloucester**, and **Edmund** enter.

KENT: I thought the king loved the Duke of Albany more than the Duke of Cornwall.

GLOUCESTER: Now that he has divided his kingdom, it's not clear which of the dukes he values most. Their shares are so equal that neither one would prefer the other's.

KENT *(indicating Edmund)***:** Isn't this your son, my lord?

GLOUCESTER: I fathered him, sir. I have so often blushed to acknowledge him that now I am hardened to it.

KENT: I cannot conceive why.

GLOUCESTER: Sir, this young fellow's mother could! So she got pregnant and had a son for her cradle before she had a husband for her bed. Do you see a fault?

KENT: I cannot wish the fault undone, the result of it being so handsome!

GLOUCESTER: But I have, sir, a legitimate son,
   older than this one, though I don't favor
   him because of that. Do you know this
   noble gentleman, Edmund?

EDMUND: No, my lord.

GLOUCESTER *(introducing him formally)*: The Lord of
   Kent, and my honorable friend.

EDMUND: At your service, my lord.

(The sound of trumpets is heard.)

GLOUCESTER: The king is coming.

(A **servant** enters, carrying a crown, followed by **King
Lear**, **the Dukes of Cornwall and Albany**, **Goneril**,
Regan, **Cordelia**, and **attendants**.)

LEAR: Bring in the lords of France and
   Burgundy, Gloucester.

GLOUCESTER: I shall, my lord.

(**Gloucester** and **Edmund** exit.)

LEAR: Meanwhile we shall reveal our plan.
   Give me that map. *(Servants bring a map.)*
   We have divided our kingdom into three parts.
   We wish to shake off all care in our old age,
   And to confer them on younger shoulders,

8

While we crawl toward death without burdens.
Tell me, my daughters, which of you
Shall we say loves us most?
Then we may be most generous where
Natural affection most deserves it. Goneril,
Our eldest child, speak first.

GONERIL: Sir, I love you more than I can say.
You are dearer than eyesight, space, and
liberty.
No less than life itself.

CORDELIA *(aside)*: What shall Cordelia say? Just
love, and be silent . . .

LEAR *(indicating Goneril's dowry on the map)*: From
    Here to here, rich with shady forests,
    Fertile plains, and teeming rivers,
    We give you to rule forever. *(turning to Regan)*
    What does our second daughter say? Speak.

REGAN: I want no other joy than
    The happiness I find in your dear love.

CORDELIA *(aside)*: Poor Cordelia, then!
    But not really so, since I am sure my love is
    Richer than my tongue can express.

LEAR: To you and your heirs, take this third
    Of our fair kingdom. No less in space, value,
    And pleasure than that given to Goneril.
    (turning to Cordelia) Now, our joy, last-born
    But not least—what can you say to attract
    A third more valuable than your sisters?
    Speak.

CORDELIA: Nothing, my lord.

LEAR: Nothing!

CORDELIA: Nothing.

LEAR: Nothing can come of nothing. Speak again.

10

CORDELIA: I cannot express what is in my heart.
  I love your majesty as a daughter should.
  No more, no less.

LEAR: What, what, Cordelia?

CORDELIA: My good lord,
  You have fathered me, taught me, loved me.
  I return those duties as I should.
  I obey you, love you, and honor you most.
  Why do my sisters have husbands
  If they say all their love is for you?
  I hope that when I marry, my husband
  Has half my love, care, and duty.

LEAR: Do these words come from your heart?

CORDELIA: Yes, my good lord.

LEAR: So young, and so hardhearted?

CORDELIA: So young, my lord, and truthful.

LEAR: Let your truth then be your dowry!
  By the sacred light of the sun, by all the stars
  That govern our lives, I hereby disown you!
  You are now a stranger to my heart and me.
  Stay away forever, my former daughter.

KENT: Your majesty—

LEAR: Silence, Kent! I loved Cordelia most
  And thought I would spend my final years
    with her. Go, out of my sight!
  My grave will be my only peace, since here
  I take her father's love from her.
  Cornwall and Albany, with my
  Two daughters' dowries, add this third:
  Let pride, which she calls truth, marry her!
  I turn over to you my power, authority, and
  All the ceremony that goes with kingship.
  We shall live with you on alternate months,
  Keeping the right to have 100 knights
  Maintained at your expense.
  We retain only the title and all the honors
    due to a king.
  Policy, taxation, and business matters,
  Beloved sons, will be yours. To confirm this,
  This crown is divided between you.

(The servant presents the crown to the dukes.)

KENT: Royal Lear, whom I have always
  Honored as my king, loved as my father—
  Kent must be rude when Lear is mad.

What are you doing, old man? Honor
   demands plain talk when kings fall to folly.
Keep your kingdom,
And think again about your rash decision.
I'll stake my life on it—your youngest
   daughter does not love you least.
Nor are they empty-hearted whose speeches
Contain no hollow flattery.

LEAR: Kent, on your life, say no more!

KENT: I do not fear losing my life when your
   safety is the goal.

LEAR: Out of my sight!

KENT: See better, Lear, and let me—as ever—
   Remain clear-sighted on your behalf.

LEAR: Hear me, traitor! Since you have tried
To make us break our vow—
Which we have never done before—hear this!
We give you five days to prepare yourself
For the troubles of the world.
On the sixth day, turn your hated back
Upon our kingdom. If you are seen here
On the tenth day—that moment is your death.
Away! By Jupiter, this will not be revoked!

KENT: Farewell, King. If this is what you want,
Freedom is elsewhere.
(to Cordelia) The gods protect you, maid.
Your thinking is right, and your words are true!
(to Regan and Goneril) May your deeds live up
to your fancy speeches.

(**Kent** exits. Trumpets announce the entry of
Gloucester, the **King of France**, the **Duke of
Burgundy**, and their **attendants**.)

LEAR: My Lord of Burgundy, we address you first.
You have been courting our daughter.
What is the least dowry you would require,
Without which you'd end your quest of love?

BURGUNDY: Most royal majesty, I beg no more
  Than your highness has already offered.

LEAR: When we loved her, we valued her more.
  Now her price has fallen.
  As she stands, she comes with our
  Displeasure, and nothing more. No dowry.
  If you want her, she is yours.

BURGUNDY *(upset)*: I don't know what to say.

LEAR: Will you take her or leave her?

BURGUNDY: Pardon me, royal sir,
  Decisions cannot be made on such terms.

LEAR: Then leave her, sir, for I'm telling you
  That's all she's worth. *(to France)* As for you,
  great king, I would not risk our friendship
  By marrying you to one I hate. So I beg you
  To turn your affection in a worthier direction.

FRANCE: This is very strange! She was so precious
  To you, the comfort of your old age.
  Suddenly she has done a thing so monstrous
  As to destroy all your affection? Your love
  Must have been false, or her offense very
  Great indeed. I could never believe that of her.

CORDELIA: I beg your majesty to make it known
  That it is no vicious deed, murder, or evil
  That has deprived me of your grace and favor.
  Rather, it is because I lack
    an eye for seeking favors and
    such a tongue that I am glad not to have.

FRANCE: Is this all? A natural shyness that often
  Keeps inner thoughts unspoken? My Lord
  Of Burgundy, what do you say to the lady?
  Love's not love when it is mixed with
    concerns that miss the entire point.
  Will you have her? She is a dowry in herself.

BURGUNDY *(to Lear)*: Royal king, just give
The dowry that you yourself proposed,
And I'll take Cordelia by the hand right now.

LEAR: I give nothing. I have sworn it.

BURGUNDY *(to Cordelia)*: I am sorry, then.
Losing a father has lost you a husband.

CORDELIA: Peace be with Burgundy!
Since he loves respectability and wealth
So much, I shall not be his wife.

FRANCE: Fairest Cordelia, you and your virtues
I here claim! If it is lawful, I will take up
What has been cast away. The gods! The gods!
It's strange that their cold neglect
Should inflame my love!
Let your penniless daughter be my queen.
Say farewell, Cordelia, though they are unkind,
You lose here to gain more elsewhere.

LEAR: Take her, France. We have no daughter,
Nor shall we ever see her face again. Go,
Without our grace, our love, or our blessing.
Come, noble Burgundy.

(**Lear, Burgundy**, **Cornwall**, **Albany**, **Gloucester**, and
attendants exit.)

FRANCE: Say goodbye to your sisters.

CORDELIA: My father's jewels, in tears I leave you.
   I know what you are, but as a sister, I hesitate
   To name your faults. I leave our father to
   Your so-called love, though
   I would prefer a better place for him.

GONERIL: Try to make your husband happy.
   He has taken you as a handout from fortune.
   You deserve what you got.

CORDELIA: Time will reveal what deceit hides.
   Those who conceal their faults are finally
      shamed. May you prosper well!

FRANCE: Come, my fair Cordelia.

(**France** and **Cordelia** exit.)

GONERIL: Sister, we have mutual interests to
   discuss. Our father will leave tonight.

REGAN: With you. Next month he'll stay with us.

GONERIL: You see how much he changes in his
      old age! He always loved our sister most.
   His poor judgment is clear
   From the way he has now cast her off.

REGAN: It's because he's so old. But then,
He has always lacked self-control.

GONERIL: Even in his prime he was hotheaded.
So now we must expect to see
Not only his lifelong faults—but new ones
That come with age and infirmity.

REGAN: No doubt we can expect sudden whims
Such as Kent's banishment.

GONERIL: And there's the rude way he said
goodbye to France! Well, then, let's work
together on this. If our father continues
to exercise his authority so rashly,
he will be a problem to us.

REGAN: We must do something—and soon!

(**Goneril** and **Regan** exit.)

Scene 2

A hall in the Earl of Gloucester's castle. **Edmund** enters, holding a letter.

EDMUND *(to himself)*: Why should society

Limit my rights, just because I am

12 or 14 months younger than my brother?

And why—just because my father didn't marry

My mother—am I considered inferior?

I am as smart and as good-looking as the son

Of any married woman. Legitimate Edgar,

I must have your inheritance! Our father

Loves me just as much as he loves you.

(waving the letter) If this letter succeeds

And my plan works, Edmund the illegitimate

Will beat Edgar the legitimate! I will prosper!

(His father, the **Earl of Gloucester**, enters.)

GLOUCESTER: Kent banished like that!

And France has left in anger!

The king has limited his own power.

All this done on a whim!

(noticing his son) Edmund, hello! What news?

EDMUND: No news, my lord.

GLOUCESTER: Why are you hiding that letter?

EDMUND: It's nothing, my lord.

GLOUCESTER: Then why hide it? Let me see.

EDMUND: I beg you, sir, pardon me. It's from my
brother, and I haven't finished it. From what
I've read so far, I find it's not fit for your eyes.

GLOUCESTER: Give me the letter, sir!

EDMUND: I hope, for my brother's sake, that he
wrote this just to test my virtue.

GLOUCESTER *(reading aloud)*: *Revering old people too much makes our best years bitter. It keeps our fortunes from us until we're too old to enjoy them! I'm beginning to feel oppressed by an aged tyrant who rules not through strength, but because I allow it. Come and see me, so I can talk to you about this. If our father would only sleep till I awakened him, you'd enjoy half his income forever, and live beloved by your brother, Edgar.*

Could he have written this? Does he have a brain to think of it? When did you get it?

EDMUND: It was thrown through my window.

GLOUCESTER: It's Edgar's handwriting!

EDMUND: I hope his heart isn't in the contents.

GLOUCESTER: Has he ever spoken of this before?

EDMUND: Never, my lord. But I have heard him say that when sons mature and fathers age, the sons should manage the money.

GLOUCESTER: Oh, the villain! That's exactly what he says in the letter. Worse than a villain! Go, sir, find him. I'll arrest him. Where is he?

EDMUND: I do not know, my lord. But I would stake my life on his honor. Perhaps he's not dangerous, but only testing my love for you.

GLOUCESTER: Do you think so?

EDMUND: If you think it's a good idea, I'll place you where you can listen to us talk about this. Then we'll both know the truth.

GLOUCESTER: He cannot be such a monster—

EDMUND: I am sure he is not.

GLOUCESTER: —to his own father, who so tenderly and entirely loves him. Edmund, find him. I must be sure of his innocence!

EDMUND: I'll find him and report back to you.

GLOUCESTER: Sound him out, Edmund— But do it carefully.

(**Gloucester** exits. A moment later, **Edgar** enters.)

EDGAR: Greetings, brother Edmund! Why do you look so grim?

EDMUND: When did you last see our father?

EDGAR: Last night.

EDMUND: Did you speak with him?

EDGAR: Yes, for two hours.

EDMUND: Did he seem displeased in any way?

EDGAR: Not at all.

EDMUND: Somehow you've offended him.
I think you'd better avoid him until
time has cooled the heat of his anger.

EDGAR: Some villain has wronged me!

EDMUND: That's what I fear. Still, I advise you to
stay away till his temper cools down. Come
with me to my place. At just the right time
I'll let you overhear what he says. Please go—
here's my key. If you do go out, go armed.

EDGAR: *Armed*, you say?

EDMUND: Brother, it's for the best. Please, go!

EDGAR: Shall I hear from you soon?

EDMUND: As soon as possible. Leave it to me.

(**Edgar** exits and Edmund talks to himself.)

A gullible father! And a noble brother
Whose very nature is so harmless
That he suspects no one. This will be easy!
I'll get my inheritance one way or the other.

(**Edmund** exits.)

24

Scene 3 🎧

A room in the Duke of Albany's palace. **Goneril** and **Oswald** enter.

GONERIL: Did my father strike my officer for
   teasing his fool?

OSWALD: Yes, madam.

GONERIL *(angry)*: I won't put up with it!
   His knights misbehave, yet he scolds us
   About every little thing. When he returns
   From hunting, I won't see him. Say I am sick.

OSWALD: He's coming, madam. I hear him.

(Hunting horns can be heard.)

GONERIL: Be as rude as you please.

    If he doesn't like it, let him go to my sister.

    We both agree not to give in to him.

    Silly old man. He thinks he can still manage

    All that he has given away!

OSWALD: Very well, madam.

GONERIL: And be cooler to his knights.

    Tell the other servants to do the same.

    I'll write to my sister at once, telling her

      to follow suit.

    Prepare for dinner.

(**They** exit.)

Scene 4 🎧

aAnother room in Albany's palace. **Kent** enters, disguised.

KENT: If I can disguise my voice as well as I have

Disguised my looks, my plan will work.

By serving in spite of being banished,

Perhaps my master, whom I love,

Will see that I am still a loyal servant.

(Hunting horns announce **Lear**'s arrival, along with his **knights** and **attendants**.)

LEAR: Well, now! Who are you?

KENT: A man, sir.

LEAR: What do you want with us?

KENT: Employment.

LEAR: With whom?

KENT: You.

LEAR: What services can you perform?

KENT: I can keep a secret, ride, run, ruin a good story by telling it, and deliver a plain message bluntly. My best quality is determination.

LEAR: Follow me. You may be my servant. If I like you no less after dinner, you can stay on permanently. (to an attendant) Get my fool.

(An **attendant** exits. **Oswald** enters.)

You, fellow, where's my daughter?

OSWALD *(brushing past him)*: Excuse me. *(He exits.)*

LEAR: What did he say? Call the blockhead back!

(A **knight** goes in pursuit.)

Where's my fool?

I think the world's asleep.

(The **knight** enters again.)

Well, now! Where's that mongrel?

KNIGHT: My lord, he says your daughter is ill.

LEAR: Why didn't he return when I called him?

KNIGHT: Sir, he rudely said that he would not.

LEAR: He would not?

KNIGHT: My lord, I don't know what's wrong— but in my opinion your highness is not being treated with the respect you once were. Duty won't allow me to be silent when your highness is being wronged.

LEAR: You are only saying aloud what I've been thinking myself. I'll look further into it. *(to attendant)* Now tell my daughter I want to see her. And call my fool here, too.

(**Attendant** exits. **Oswald** enters again.)

You. Come here, sir. Who am I, sir?

OSWALD: My lady's father.

LEAR: "My lady's father!" You lousy dog! Wretch!

OSWALD: I am none of these, my lord.

LEAR: Do you contradict me, you rascal?

(He strikes Oswald angrily.)

OSWALD: I'll not be struck, my lord.

KENT *(tripping him):* Nor tripped either, I suppose?

(Oswald falls to the ground.)

LEAR *(to Kent):* I thank you, fellow. You're my servant, and I'll take care of you.

KENT *(to Oswald):* Come on, sir, get up! I'll teach you your place! Go!

(He pushes **Oswald** out.)

LEAR: Now, my loyal new servant, I thank you. Here's something for your service.

(Lear gives Kent money. The **fool** enters.)

LEAR: Hello, my pretty fellow. How are you?

FOOL *(to Kent)*: Sir, you'd better take my cap.

(The fool offers Kent his jester's cap.)

KENT: Why, fool?

FOOL: Why, for siding with someone who is out
   of favor! If you don't side with the winners,
   you'll soon be out in the cold.

LEAR: Be careful, sir, or you'll be whipped!

FOOL: Truth's a dog that's sent to his kennel.
   He gets whipped. But flattery, the mongrel
      dog, is allowed to stand by the fire and stink.

LEAR *(remembering how he banished Cordelia for
   telling the truth)*: A bitter cup for me!

FOOL: Do you know the difference
   Between a bitter fool and a sweet one?

LEAR: No, lad. Tell me.

FOOL: The lord who advised you
   To give away your land,
   Come place him here by me.
   You may stand in his place.

30

The sweet and bitter fool
Will presently appear.
The one in fool's clothes here—
The other one standing there!
(He points to Lear as the bitter one.)

LEAR: Do you call me a *fool*, boy?

FOOL: You have given away all your other titles—
That one you were born with.

KENT: He's not all fool, my lord.

FOOL: No, indeed. Uncle, give me an egg, and
I'll give you two crowns.

LEAR: What two crowns would they be?

FOOL: Why, after I have cut the egg in half and eaten the yolk, the two halves of the eggshell! Remember when you chopped your crown in the middle and gave away both parts? You had little sense in your bald crown when you gave your golden one away. If I'm speaking like a fool here, whip the man who first finds it so.

LEAR: If you are lying, sir, you'll be whipped.

FOOL: I marvel at how alike you and your daughters are. They'll have me whipped for speaking the truth, and you'll have me whipped for lying! I'd rather be anything else but a fool. But I would not want to be you, uncle. You have sliced your brains in two and left nothing in the middle. Look! Here comes one of the halves.

(**Goneril** enters.)

LEAR: Well, daughter. Why the frowning face?

GONERIL: All of your rude followers are
Bickering and quarreling by the hour.
They break out into riots. I thought you'd
Do something when I first told you.

But now it looks as if you not only allow

This behavior, but encourage it.

LEAR: Are you really our daughter?

GONERIL: Come, sir! I wish you would use

The common sense I know you still have,

And stop behaving as you've been doing lately.

LEAR: Does anyone here know me?

Does Lear walk this way? Speak this way?

Can anyone here tell me who I am?

I'd really like to know! From the evidence

Of knowledge and reason, I'd be misled

Into thinking I had daughters.

GONERIL: This spectacle, sir, is on the same order

As your other pranks. Please understand me.

As you are old and respected, be wise.

Here you keep 100 knights and squires.

These men are so disorderly, drunk, and bold

That our court—influenced by their actions—

Looks like a rowdy inn. It is more like a tavern

Than a gracious palace. This must be stopped!

I urge you to reduce the

Size of your retinue by half.

Keep the ones who are closer to your age—
Those who can control themselves and you.

LEAR: Darkness and devils! Saddle my horses!
Call my men together! You ungrateful wretch!
I'll not trouble you any longer.
I still have one daughter left!

(**Albany** enters.)

Oh, sir, so you're here! Is this your doing?
Speak, sir. *(to his servants)* Prepare my horses.

ALBANY: Please, sir, settle down.

LEAR *(to Goneril)***:** Vulture! You tell lies!
My troops are men of rare value.
They know their duties and act honorably.

34

Oh, how such a small fault in Cordelia
Seemed so ugly! It drew love from my heart,
　making me bitter.

(**Kent** and the **knights** exit.)

ALBANY: My lord, I am as guiltless
　As I am ignorant of what has upset you.

LEAR: It may be so, my lord. *(turning to Goneril)*
　How sharper than a serpent's tooth it is
　To have a thankless child!

(**Lear** exits, overcome with emotion.)

ALBANY: Where did that come from?

GONERIL: Don't bother yourself to find out.
　Let his moods be ruled by his old age.

(**Lear** enters again.)

LEAR: What, 50 of my followers all at once?
　Within two weeks?

ALBANY: What's the matter, sir?

LEAR: I'll tell you. *(to Goneril)* Life and death!
　I am ashamed that you can shake my
　Manly dignity like this, as if you are worthy
　Of these hot tears, which burst from me.
　Storms and fogs upon you!

May the deep wounds of a father's curse
Pierce every one of your senses.
Foolish old eyes, if you cry any more,
I'll pluck you out and trample you!
Has it really come to this? Let it be so.
I have another daughter! I am sure
That she is kind and comforting.

(**Lear**, **Kent**, and **attendants** exit.)

GONERIL: Did you see that?

ALBANY: For all the great love I have for you,
  Goneril, I cannot believe that—

GONERIL *(stopping him)*: That's enough.
  (calling out) Oswald! Come here!
  (to the fool) Go after your master.

FOOL: Uncle Lear, take the fool with you!

(The **fool** runs off after Lear.)

GONERIL *(sarcastically)*: My father has been
  well-advised. One hundred knights! Indeed!
  After every complaint or dislike, he can
  Back up his senile ways with their powers,
  And hold our lives at his mercy.

ALBANY: Well, you may be worrying too much.

GONERIL: That's safer than trusting too much.

I know his heart. I've written to my sister

About what he has said. If she lets him and

His 100 knights stay,

After I've explained what a bad idea it is—

(**Oswald** enters again.)

Well, now, Oswald!

Do you have that letter to my sister?

OSWALD: Yes, madam.

GONERIL: Take some men with you and ride off.

Tell her fully of my particular fears, and add

Such reasons of your own to convince her.

Go now, and hurry back!

(**Oswald** exits.)

This gentle attitude of yours,

My lord, though I do not condemn it—

I do disagree with it.

ALBANY: How far you are right, I cannot tell.

Sometimes it's best to leave things alone.

GONERIL: Well, then.

ALBANY: Well, well. We'll see what happens.

(**They** exit.)

Scene 5 🎧(7)

A room in the Duke of Albany's palace. **Lear**, **Kent**, and the **fool** enter.

LEAR: Go to Gloucester with this letter.

KINT: I will not sleep until I've delivered it.

(**Kent** exits.)

FOOL: You'll see your other daughter will treat you the same way. I can tell what I can tell.

LEAR: What can you tell, boy?

FOOL: I can tell you why a snail has a house.

LEAR: Why?

FOOL: To put his head in—not to give it to his daughters and leave himself homeless.

LEAR: So kind a father! Are my horses ready?

FOOL: Your men are preparing them.

LEAR: I'll take my kingdom back again!

FOOL: If you were my fool, uncle, I'd have you beaten for being old before your time.

LEAR: What do you mean?

FOOL: You shouldn't have grown old until you were wise.

LEAR: Oh, let me not be mad, sweet heaven! Keep me sane. I don't want to be mad!

(A **gentleman** enters.)

Are the horses ready?

GENTLEMAN: Ready, my lord.

LEAR *(to the fool)*: Come, boy.

(**They** exit.)

ACT 2

Summary

艾德加落入艾德蒙所設的陷阱,使得葛勞塞斯特不再承認他是自己的兒子,艾德加不得不逃跑。里根和康沃爾加入艾德蒙的背叛詭計,他們假裝與葛勞塞斯特為友,並請他幫忙處理李爾王的「麻煩」。接著貢納莉的信差奧斯華因與貢納莉同夥對付李爾王,被偽裝的肯特攻擊。為了替奧斯華平反,里根和康沃爾將肯特套上刑具,此舉惹怒葛勞塞斯特。

在此期間,被貢納莉無理對待的李爾王請求里根接待他與他的守衛。但貢納莉出現時,兩姊妹卻親切地彼此招呼,而李爾王發現她的女兒皆不願意接待他與他的隨從,甚至合夥要反抗他。在極度絕望中,李爾王走進暴風雨,為他的悲慘處境痛哭。

Scene 1 🎧

The Earl of Gloucester's castle. **Edmund** and
Curan enter.

CURAN: I have told your father that the Duke of
Cornwall and Regan will be here tonight.

EDMUND: How has that come about?

CURAN: I don't know. Have you heard the rumors?

EDMUND: No. What are they?

CURAN: You haven't heard of the likely wars
between the Dukes of Cornwall and Albany?

EDMUND: Not a word.

CURAN: You will soon, no doubt. Farewell, sir.

(**Curan** exits.)

EDMUND: The duke will be here tonight? Great!
This fits in with my plan. My father
Has hidden himself to overhear my brother.
(Seeing Edgar enter, from a staircase.) I have one
thing to do first. Brother, a word!
(to the audience) My father is watching!
(to Edgar, in a whisper) Sir, run away!
Your hiding place has been found out.
Haven't you been speaking against Cornwall?

He's coming here tonight, with Regan.

Have you said anything

To support his argument with Albany?

EDGAR: No, not a word.

EDMUND: I hear my father coming. Pardon me.

I must pretend to draw my sword on you.

(He draws.) Draw yours. Pretend to fight.

(Edgar, confused, does as he is told.)

Do your best! *(loudly, so Gloucester can hear)*
Surrender!

(They continue to pretend to fight. Edmund whispers to Edgar.)

Run now, brother. Farewell!

(**Edgar** runs off.)

Some blood on me would hint
That I had a tough struggle. *(He cuts his arm.)*
Father! Father! *(calling after Edgar)* Stop! Stop!
Will no one help?

(**Gloucester** enters, with **servants** carrying torches.)

GLOUCESTER: Now, Edmund, where's the villain?

EDMUND: Look, sir, I'm bleeding!

GLOUCESTER: Where is the villain, Edmund?

EDMUND *(pointing)*: He ran that way, sir.

GLOUCESTER: Follow him, quick! Go!

(**Servants** exit, running after Edgar.)

EDMUND: He tried to get me to murder you,
    But I told him the revenging gods were harsh
    With those who killed their fathers.
    When he saw how firmly I was against his plan,
    He drew his sword and cut my arm.
    Then I defended myself, and he ran off.

GLOUCESTER: No matter how far he runs,
    Nowhere in this land shall he remain free.
    He'll be found and killed!

EDMUND: When I said I'd expose him,

He said, "Who would believe you?

I'd deny everything and blame it on you—

even if you produced my own handwriting!

Any idiot could see that you would profit

from my death."

GLOUCESTER: He's no son of mine!

I'll send that villain's picture

Far and near, for all the kingdom to see.

And I'll arrange for you, loyal and true son,

to inherit my lands.

(Trumpets are heard.)

Listen! The duke's trumpets.

(**Cornwall**, **Regan**, and **attendants** enter.)

CORNWALL: Greetings, my noble friend!

I've just heard some strange news.

REGAN: If it's true, no vengeance is too great.

How are you, my lord?

GLOUCESTER: Madam, my old heart is broken!

REGAN: Did my father's godson seek your life?

Was it your Edgar?

GLOUCESTER: Shame would have it hidden!

REGAN: Was he with the riotous knights
    Who served my father?

GLOUCESTER: I don't know, madam.

EDMUND: Yes, madam, he was with them.

REGAN: No wonder then that he was so disloyal.
    They want him to plan the old man's death
    So he can spend the old man's wealth.
    Just this evening my sister told me about
      them—
    With such warnings that if they come
    To stay with me, I won't be there.

CORNWALL: Nor I, Regan, I assure you.
    Edmund, I hear that you have been a good
      son to your father.

EDMUND: It was my duty, sir.

GLOUCESTER: He exposed Edgar's plot and got
This wound you see, trying to arrest him.

CORNWALL: Is Edgar being pursued?

GLOUCESTER: Yes, my good lord.

CORNWALL: If he is caught, never fear him again.
Use my resources as you please. As for you,
Edmund, you shall be one of us from now on.
Such loyal, trustworthy men are always needed.

EDMUND *(bowing):* I am at your service, sir.

CORNWALL: We are here on an important matter.

REGAN: Our father has written—
So has our sister—about certain quarrels.
I want to answer him away from home.
The messengers are waiting to be sent.
Our good old friend, give us your
Much-needed advice about this business.

GLOUCESTER: I serve you, madam.

(Trumpets sound as **all** exit.)

Scene ❷

ACT 2
SCENE 2

Before Gloucester's castle. **Kent** and **Oswald** meet.

KENT: I know you, man. You are a knave, a
rascal, and a coward!

OSWALD: Why, what a monstrous fellow you are,
to say that to someone you don't even know!

KENT: What a scoundrel you are to deny
knowing me! Isn't it just two days
since I beat you and tripped you before
the king? Draw your sword, you rogue!
(drawing his sword) Draw!

OSWALD: Go! I'll have nothing to do with you!

KENT: Draw, you rascal! You're here with letters
against the king, and you take your lady's side
against her royal father. Draw, you rogue!

OSWALD: Help! Murder! Help!

KENT: Fight, you coward! Fight!

(Kent beats Oswald with the broad side of his sword.)

OSWALD: Help! Murder! Murder!

(**Edmund**, **Cornwall**, **Regan**, **Gloucester**, and
servants enter.)

47

GLOUCESTER: Weapons! Fighting! What's all this?

REGAN: They are the messengers from our sister
and the king.

CORNWALL: What is your quarrel? Speak.

KENT: No two men hate each other more than
that rogue and I.

CORNWALL *(to Oswald)*: What did you do to him?

OSWALD: Nothing. A recent misunderstanding
Made him trip me. When I fell, he insulted me.
Then he made himself out to be such a hero
That the king praised him for tackling a man
Who wasn't putting up a fight. Inspired by
His earlier success, he drew on me here again.

CORNWALL: Bring the stocks here!
You stubborn rogue, we'll teach you!

KENT: Sir, I am too old to learn. Don't call
Your stocks for me. I serve the king.
In putting his messenger in the stocks,
You would be showing disrespect to the king.

CORNWALL: Get the stocks! Upon my word,
He shall sit there till noon.

REGAN: Till noon? Till *night*, my lord!

48

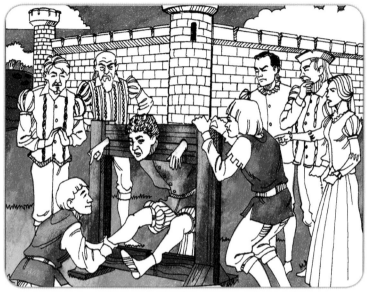

KENT: Why, madam, if I were your father's dog,
    You wouldn't treat me like that.

REGAN: Sir, since you're his knave, I will.

(**Servants** carry the stocks in.)

GLOUCESTER: I beg your grace not to do this.
    He's at fault, and the king will punish him.
    The stocks are for thieves and other wretches.

CORNWALL: I'll answer for that.

REGAN: My sister might not like to hear
    That her servant Oswald was so abused
    For carrying out her business. Put his legs in.

(Kent is put in the stocks.)

CORNWALL: Let's go, my lord.

(**All** but Gloucester and Kent exit.)

GLOUCESTER: I'm sorry for you, friend.
It's the duke's whim. Everyone knows
How stubborn he is. I'll plead for you.

KENT: Please do not, sir. Some of the time
I'll sleep, and the rest I'll whistle.
Even a good man sometimes has bad luck.
Good day to you!

GLOUCESTER: The duke's at fault for this.
It will be taken badly.

(**Gloucester** exits.)

KENT: I know that Cordelia's been told about
My disguise. She will find the best time to
Set things right in this monstrous state.
Do not look, heavy eyes, upon these
Shameful stocks. Good night, Fortune! Smile
Once more, and then turn your wheel!

(He sleeps.)

Scene ❸ 🎧

The open country. **Edgar** enters, talking to himself.

EDGAR: Hearing myself called an outlaw,

I escaped the hunt in this hollow tree.

No seaport is free. Every place is

Tightly guarded to trap me.

While I can still escape, I'll disguise myself.

I'll cover my face with filth,

Wear rags, and mat all my hair in knots.

This country is full of lunatic beggars with

Roaring voices, who stick pins, skewers,

And nails into their bare arms. Then they beg

From humble farms and poor villages,

Using lunatic curses and prayers.

(He speaks like a mad beggar.) Poor Tom!

(in his normal voice) That's what's left for me.

As Edgar, I'm nothing.

(**Edgar** exits.)

Scene 4

Before Gloucester's castle. **Kent** is in the stocks. **Lear** and the **fool** enter.

LEAR: It's strange that they should leave home
Like that and not send back my messenger.

GENTLEMAN: I heard their leaving was sudden.

KENT: Greetings, noble master!

LEAR: What, is this sort of shame your hobby?

KENT: No, my lord.

LEAR: Who put you here?

KENT: Two people—your son and your daughter.

LEAR: They wouldn't. They couldn't ! It's worse
Than murder to do such an outrage
Against an officer of the king.

KENT: My lord, when I gave your letters to them
Another messenger arrived at their home.
He was half breathless, panting greetings from
His mistress Goneril. He delivered letters
Which they read at once.
After that, they summoned their servants
And immediately took to their horses.

They commanded me to follow and wait for a
Reply at their leisure. They gave me cold looks.
I met the other messenger here. I realized that
His welcome had poisoned mine.
He was the same fellow who had recently been
So disrespectful to your highness.
Having more courage than sense,
I drew my sword. He called out
With loud and cowardly cries.
Your son and daughter found this action
Worth the shame I'm now suffering.

LEAR: Oh, how sorrow swells my heart!

Where is this daughter?

KENT: With the duke, sir, indoors.

LEAR: I will go speak to her.

(**Lear** exits.)

FOOL: You could learn a lesson from the ant—
there's nothing to be gained from working
for a lost cause. Don't hold on to a huge
wheel that's running down a hill—you
might break your neck trying to keep up
with it. When a wise man gives you better
advice, return mine.

(**Lear** enters again, with **Gloucester**.)

LEAR: Refused to speak with me! They say they
    Are weary and sick?
    They have traveled all night? Mere excuses—
    The symbols of revolt and desertion.
    Bring me a better answer.

GLOUCESTER: My dear lord,
    You know how stubborn the Duke is.

LEAR: Stubborn? Why, Gloucester, I want to
    Speak with the Duke of Cornwall and his wife.

GLOUCESTER: Well, my good lord, I have
    informed them so.

LEAR: "Informed" them! Do you understand me?

GLOUCESTER: Yes, my good lord.

LEAR: The king wishes to speak with Cornwall.
    The dear father wishes to speak with his
    Daughter. I command her obedience.
    Have they both been informed of this?
    My breath and blood!
    (looking at Kent in the stocks and getting angrier)
    Death to my royal power! Why should he sit here?
    I want my servant out of the stocks!

Go tell the duke and his wife that I demand
To speak with them now!

(**Gloucester** exits.)

LEAR: Oh, me! My heart is rising! But, down!

FOOL: Give it its orders, uncle, as the cook did to
the eels when she put them in the pan alive.
She hit them with a stick and cried,
"Down, you creatures, *down*!"

(**Cornwall**, **Regan**, **Gloucester**, and **servants** enter.
Kent is set free.)

REGAN: I am glad to see your highness.

LEAR: Regan, I know you are.
(to Kent) Oh, are you free? We'll discuss this
Some other time. *(Kent leaves.)*
Beloved Regan, your sister is wicked.
Her sharp-toothed unkindness has eaten
At my heart like a vulture. Oh, Regan!

REGAN: I beg you, sir, be patient. I cannot believe
My sister would fail in her obligation to you.
If she has calmed the riotous actions of your
Followers, she should be praised, not blamed.

LEAR: My curses on her!

REGAN: Oh, sir, you are old and close to the end
  of your life.
   You should be led by someone wise
     who knows you
   Better than you know yourself.
   Therefore, I beg you, return to our sister.
   Say you have wronged her, sir.

LEAR: Ask her forgiveness?
   See how this looks for royalty! *(He kneels.)*
   "Dear Daughter, I confess that I am old.
   Age is a nuisance. On my knees I beg
   That you'll give me clothing, a bed, and food."

REGAN: Good sir, no more of this!
   These are ugly tricks. Return to my sister.

LEAR *(rising):* Never, Regan!
   She has deprived me of half my retinue,
   Given me dark looks, and spoken rudely.
   May the gods strike her bones with lameness!

REGAN: Oh, the gods! Will you curse me, too,
   When you're in a bad mood?

LEAR: No, Regan, you shall never have my curse.
   Your tender nature would never turn harsh.
   Her eyes are fierce, but yours are warm.

It is not in you to begrudge me my pleasures.
You know how to be grateful.
You haven't forgotten the half of the kingdom
That I gave to you.

REGAN: Good sir, get to the point.

LEAR: Who put my man in the stocks?

(A trumpet sounds.)

CORNWALL: Whose trumpet is that?

REGAN: It is my sister's. She said in her letter
That she would be here soon.

(**Oswald** enters.)

Has your lady arrived?

LEAR (*frowning at Oswald*): This is the wretch who
Put my servant in the stocks! Regan,
I trust you did not know about it.

(**Goneril** approaches.)

Who's that? Oh, heavens!
If you love old men, help me now!
(*to Goneril*) Aren't you ashamed of yourself?
(*The sisters embrace.*) Oh, Regan, will you hold
her hand?

GONERIL: Why not my hand, sir? How have I
offended you?

57

LEAR *(holding his heart)*: Is there no end to this?
(to Cornwall) Why was my man in the stocks?

CORNWALL: I put him there, sir.
His own conduct deserved worse.

LEAR: You! Did you?

REGAN: Father, being weak, act accordingly.
Return and stay with my sister for the rest of
The month—dismissing half your guards—
And then come to me.

LEAR: Return to her, and dismiss 50 men?
No, I would rather reject all shelter and fight
The elements, be friends with wolves and owls.
Return with her? Why, I could just as easily
Kneel at France's throne and,
Like a poor squire, beg for a pension to live on!
Return with her? Ask me rather to be a slave
To this hated servant. *(He points to Oswald.)*

GONERIL: It's your choice, sir.

LEAR: I beg you, daughter, do not make me mad.
I will not trouble you, my child. Farewell.
We'll meet no more, see each other no more.
But still you are my flesh and blood,

Or rather a disease in my flesh, like a boil,

A plague sore, a swollen tumor in my blood!

　　But I'll not scold you. Shame will come to

　　you in its own time.

I can be patient. I can stay with Regan—

I and my 100 knights.

REGAN: Not quite. I wasn't expecting you yet,

　　And I am not prepared for a fitting welcome.

　　Listen to my sister. She's right.

LEAR: Are you sure?

REGAN: Absolutely, sir. What, 50 followers?

　　Isn't that enough? Why should you need more?

　　How can so many people live in one house,

　　Under two commands, and get along?

GONERIL: Why couldn't you, my lord, be served

　　By her servants, or by mine?

REGAN: Why not, my lord? If they neglected you,

　　We could correct them. If you come to me,

　　I would ask you to bring only 25. I'll take care of

　　　no more than that.

LEAR: What? I gave you everything—

REGAN: And you took your time about it!

LEAR: —but on the condition that I should have
100 knights in my retinue. What?
Must I come to you with 25? Regan,
Is that what you said?

REGAN: And I say it again. No more with me.

LEAR: Some wicked creatures look good
Compared to others who are more wicked.
(to Goneril) I'll go with you. Your 50
Is double her 25, so your love is double hers.

GONERIL: Hear me, my lord, why do you need
25, 10, or even 5 to serve you in a house
Where twice as many are at your service?

REGAN: What need do you have of one?

LEAR: Don't talk about need.
Even the poorest beggars
Have something they could do without.
If you allow no more than one needs,
Our lives would be no better than a beast's.
If you dressed only for warmth,
You'd not need those pretty clothes
That scarcely keep you warm. Heavens!
Give me the patience that I need!
You see me here, you gods, a poor old man,

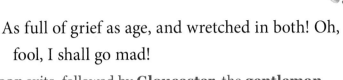

As full of grief as age, and wretched in both! Oh,

fool, I shall go mad!

(**Lear** exits, followed by **Gloucester**, the **gentleman**, and the **fool**. A storm is heard in the distance.)

CORNWALL: Let's go in. A storm is coming.

REGAN: This house is too little for the old man

and his people.

GONERIL: It's his own fault. He's upset himself,

So he must suffer for his own foolishness.

REGAN: By himself, I'll receive him gladly.

But not one follower.

GONERIL: I feel the same way.

(**Gloucester** enters again.)

GLOUCESTER: The king is in a terrible rage.

GONERIL: My lord, by no means beg him to stay.

GLOUCESTER: But night's coming, and it's stormy.

REGAN: Willful men learn from their own errors.

Shut your doors. His followers are desperate.

Who knows what they'll provoke him to do?

CORNWALL: Shut your doors. It's a wild night.

Regan's right. Come out of the storm.

(**All** exit.)

ACT 3

Summary

打扮成僕人的肯特伯爵,發現李爾王
和傻子在滂沱大雨中的荒野遊蕩,他將國王帶至附近的棚
子躲避風雨,他們遇見假扮成發瘋乞丐窮酸湯姆的艾德加。
葛勞塞斯特出現,他不願服從國王女兒們「嚴苛的命令」,
而向李爾王表示忠誠。同時,艾德蒙讓康沃爾讀一封信,證
明葛勞塞斯特在暗助法王,而他已為英格蘭的敵人。

此時,葛勞塞斯特和仍繼續偽裝的肯特,與李爾王和傻子在
農舍見面,李爾王對其女兒們的惡行進行一場假審判,李爾
王指派傻子和肯特擔任審判官。當李爾王怒言相向,肯特發
現李爾王已失去自制力,請求他歇息片刻。接著,葛勞塞斯
特說他無意間側聽到有人密謀要殺國王,葛勞塞斯特和其
他人將李爾王抬去多佛,法軍軍營駐紮之處。

聽到李爾王身在多佛的消息,邪惡的康沃爾將葛勞塞斯特逮
捕並弄瞎他。當僕人試圖阻止其暴行,里根一劍刺死了他,
並命令將瞎眼的葛勞塞斯特逐出大門外。有兩名僕人可憐
葛勞塞斯特,將他交給仍假扮成窮酸湯姆的艾德加照顧。

Scene ❶ 🎧⑫

A heath during a storm. Thunder and lightning. **Kent** and a **gentleman** enter.

KENT: Where's the king?

GENTLEMAN: Dealing with the angry elements.
He tells the wind to blow the earth into the sea,
Or raise the waves over the mainland. He tears
His white hair, which the wind whips about.
He tries to out-storm the wind and rain.
Tonight—when even bears, lions, and wolves
Take cover from the storm—he runs
   bareheaded
And cries out desperately.

KENT: But who is with him?

GENTLEMAN: Only the fool.

KENT: Sir, I'll tell you something important.
Although they hide it, a division exists
Between Albany and Cornwall.
They have servants who seem loyal, but
Who are actually spies for the King of France.
These servants supply information about the
   dukes' quarrels and the shameful way they

Have treated the kind old king. The truth is
That an army has come from France
To this divided kingdom. They have already
Arrived secretly at some of our best ports.
If you hurry to Dover, you shall find
   men there
Who will thank you for a true report of
The king's unnatural and maddening sorrow.
I am a gentleman of noble blood and breeding,
And I tell you this on reliable information.
To prove that I am more than I appear to be,
Open this purse and take what is in it.
When you see Cordelia, show her this ring.
She will tell you who I am.
Damn this storm! Let's go find the king.
You go that way, and I'll go this.
Whoever sees him first, holler to the other.

(**Both** exit.)

Scene ❷ 🎧⑬

Another part of the heath. Storm continues. **Lear** and the **fool** enter.

LEAR: Blow, winds, and crack your cheeks!

Rage! Blow! You blasts of lightning,

Singe my white head!

FOOL: Oh, uncle, flattery in a dry house

Is better than this rain outside! Go in—

And ask for a blessing from your daughters.

This night pities neither wise men nor fools.

LEAR: Spit, fire! Spout, rain! Rain, wind,
Thunder, fire—they're not my daughters!
I do not accuse you elements of unkindness.
I never gave you a kingdom or called you
children.
You owe me nothing. So do as you will!

(**Kent** enters, in disguise.)

KENT: Alas, sir, are you here? Even creatures
That love night do not love nights like these.
The angry skies frighten even the wildest
animals
And make them stay in their caves.
I've never seen such a storm!

LEAR: Let the great gods, who are making
This dreadful noise over our heads, Identify their
enemies now.
(*He removes his hat to show he has nothing to fear.*)
I am a man more sinned against than sinning.

KENT: Alas, bareheaded!
My gracious lord, a nearby shed will
give you some shelter from the storm.

I will return to your cruel house and force
Its hardhearted occupants to be courteous.

LEAR: Where is this shed, my fellow?
Need is a strange thing. It can make lowly
Things precious. Lead on, to the shed.

(**They** exit.)

Scene ❸ 〔14〕

A room in Gloucester's castle. **Gloucester** and **Edmund** enter, carrying torches.

GLOUCESTER: This behavior is unnatural! They've ordered me never to speak of him, plead for him, or in any way help him.

EDMUND: Most savage and unnatural!

GLOUCESTER: *Sh!* Say nothing. The dukes have quarreled. And here's something worse: I received a letter tonight. It's dangerous to speak of it. I have locked the letter in my bedroom. These wrongs the king has suffered will be avenged in full. Part of an army has already landed. We must take the king's side. I will find him and secretly help him. Keep the duke talking, Edmund, so he won't notice I'm gone. If he asks for me, say I am sick in bed. Even if I die for it, I must help the king. Strange things are sure to happen. Please be careful, Edmund.

(**Gloucester** goes to look for Lear.)

EDMUND: I'll tell the duke about this—
And about that letter, too. I will gain
What my father loses—no less than all!
The young rise when the old fall.
(**Edmund** exits.)

Scene 4 15

The heath, in front of the shed. The storm continues. **Lear**, **Kent** (still disguised), and the **fool** enter.

KENT: Here is the place, my lord. Enter.

LEAR: You think it matters that this storm
Soaks us to the skin. So it does, to you.
But where there is greater suffering,
  lesser suffering is hardly felt.
The storm in my mind
Takes all feeling from my senses
Except what's tormenting me—
The ingratitude of my daughters!
It's as if my mouth would bite my hand
For lifting food to it. I'll punish thoroughly!
But, I will weep no more.
To shut me out on a night like this!
(to the storm) Pour on—I can take it!
Oh, Regan! Goneril! Your kind old father,
Whose open heart gave you everything!

KENT: My good lord, enter here.

LEAR *(to the fool)*: In, boy. You go first.
I'll pray, and then I'll sleep.

(The **fool** goes in.)

EDGAR *(from inside the shed, pretending to be insane)*:
Poor Tom! Poor Tom!

(The **fool** runs out.)

FOOL: Don't go there, uncle. There's a ghost!
He says his name's Poor Tom.

KENT: Who are you in the shed? Come out.

(**Edgar** appears, disguised as a madman.)

EDGAR: Go away! The foul fiend follows me!

LEAR: Did you give everything to your daughters?

EDGAR: Who gives anything to poor Tom?
The foul fiend leads him through fire
and swamps. He's put knives under
his pillow and poison by his soup.
(He swipes at an imaginary attacker.) I could
catch him now—and there—and there again!

(The storm rages on.)

LEAR: Have his daughters brought him to this?
Could you save nothing? Did you give
them all?

FOOL: He saved a blanket, which is all he wears.

LEAR: May all the plagues that hang in the air
Land on your daughters!

KENT: He has no daughters, sir.

LEAR: Nothing could have brought him
To such lowness but his unkind daughters!
Is it the fashion now for discarded fathers
To endure such sufferings of the flesh?
How just the punishment!
It was this very flesh
That conceived those father-killing daughters!

FOOL: This cold night will turn us all to
fools and madmen. *(He sees Gloucester
approaching, carrying a torch.)* Look, here comes
a walking fire!

LEAR *(peering in the dark)*: Who are you?

GLOUCESTER: My lord, I am here to help.
Come with me. My sense of duty
Forbids me to obey your daughters'
Harsh commands. Their order is
To bar my doors, and let this pitiless night
Take its hold on you. But I have come to
Bring you to where fire and food are ready.

KENT: Ask him again,

My lord. His mind is failing.

GLOUCESTER: Can you blame him?

His daughters want him dead.

Ah, that good Kent! He said it would be thus.

The poor, banished man!

You say the king grows mad. I'll tell you,

Friend, I am almost mad myself. I had a son,

Now disowned. He sought my life,

Only recently! I loved him, friend—

No father loved a son more. In truth,

The grief has driven me almost crazy.

(The storm rages.) What a night this is!

(to Lear) I do beg your grace—

EDGAR: Tom's so cold.

GLOUCESTER: In, fellow, into the shed! Get warm.

LEAR: Come. Let's all go in.

(They all enter the shed.)

Scene 5 16

A room in Gloucester's castle. **Cornwall** and **Edmund** enter. Cornwall is waving a letter.

CORNWALL: I see now that it was not just your brother's evil nature that made him seek your father's death. He was provoked into it by your father's treason.

EDMUND: Here's the letter my father mentioned. It proves him to be acting on behalf of France. Oh, heavens! If only this treason had never happened—or that I wasn't the one to discover it! If the contents of this letter are true, you have important business to do.

CORNWALL *(having read the letter)*: True or false, it has made you the Earl of Gloucester. Find your father, so we may arrest him.

EDMUND *(aside)*: If I find my father helping the king, it will make the duke even more suspicious. *(aloud)* I will continue to be loyal, though it conflicts with my feelings as a son.

CORNWALL: I will trust in you, and I promise that you shall find a more loving father in me.

(**They** exit.)

A room in a farmhouse near the castle. **Gloucester** and **Kent** (disguised) enter.

ACT 3
SCENE
6

GLOUCESTER: This is better than the open air.

Let's try to make it more comfortable yet.

I won't be away for long.

KENT: His mind is completely gone under the

stress. May the gods reward your kindness!

(**Gloucester** exits. **Edgar**, the **fool**, and **Lear** enter.)

LEAR: I will punish those ungrateful daughters!

(to Edgar) Come, sit here. You're a judge.

(to the fool) You, wise sir, sit here. You're

another judge.

(to Kent) And you—sit down, too.

(rubbing his hands) Now, you she-foxes!

EDGAR *(pointing to Lear):* Look how he glares!

KENT: How are you, sir? Don't be dismayed.

Won't you lie down and rest on these cushions?

LEAR: I'll see their trial first. Bring the witnesses.

EDGAR: Let us have a fair trial.

LEAR *(pointing to an empty seat)*: Prosecute her first.
It's Goneril. I say under my oath before this
honorable assembly that she kicked the
king, her poor father.

FOOL: Come here. Is your name Goneril?

LEAR: She cannot deny it.

FOOL: I'm sorry. I mistook you for a stool!

LEAR: And here's another one, whose ugly looks
Reveal what her heart is made of.
(He jumps up excitedly.) Stop her there!
(to Edgar) False judge! You let her escape!

KENT: Oh, for pity! Sir, where is the self-control
You have so often claimed to have?

EDGAR *(aside, as himself)*: My tears of sympathy
For him are going to ruin my disguise.

LEAR: The little dogs—see, they bark at me.
Let them dissect Regan. See what festers
about her heart. Is there any cause in
nature that makes their hearts so hard?

KENT: Now, my lord, lie here and rest awhile.

LEAR *(as if at home in bed)*: Make no noise. Draw the
curtains. We'll go to supper in the morning.

(**Gloucester** enters again.)

GLOUCESTER *(to Kent)*: Where is the king?

KENT: Don't bother him, sir. His mind is gone.

GLOUCESTER: Good friend, I beg of you,
Take him in your arms. I have overheard
A plot to kill him. There's a stretcher ready.
Lay him on it, and take him to Dover.
There you'll be welcomed and protected.

KENT: Stress has worn him out, and he sleeps.
(to the fool) Come, help me carry him.

GLOUCESTER: Come, come away!

(**Kent**, **Gloucester**, and the **fool** carry **Lear** out.)

EDGAR: When we see our betters suffering,
Our own miseries are easier to bear.
He suffers from his children,
As I do from my father! Tom, away!
Throw off your disguise when you are cleared
Of the false charges that shame you.
Whatever else happens tonight,
May the king escape safely!
Until then, stay in hiding.

(**Edgar** exits.)

Scene 7

A room in Gloucester's castle. **Cornwall**, **Regan**, **Goneril**, **Edmund**, and **servants** enter.

CORNWALL *(to Goneril)*: Send a messenger with this letter to my lord, your husband. France's army has landed. Find the traitor Gloucester!

(Some **servants** leave.)

REGAN: Hang him instantly!

GONERIL: Pluck out his eyes!

CORNWALL: Leave him to my displeasure. Edmund, stay with Goneril. The revenge we are planning to take on your traitorous father is not fit for you to behold. Tell the duke, when you see him, to prepare for war. We'll do the same.

(**Oswald** enters.)

Well, where's the king?

OSWALD: My Lord of Gloucester
Has taken him away. Some 30 of his knights
And several of Lord Gloucester's men
Met him at the gate. They all went to Dover,
Where they claim to have well-armed friends.

CORNWALL: Get horses for your mistress.

GONERIL: Farewell, sweet lord, and sister.

CORNWALL: Edmund, farewell.

(**Goneril**, **Edmund**, and **Oswald** leave.)

Go and find the traitor Gloucester.
Tie him up like a thief, and bring him to us.

(Other **servants** exit.)

Though we cannot condemn him to death
Without a trial, we can indulge our anger.
Anger may be blamed but not controlled.
Who's there? The traitor?

(**Servants** enter with **Gloucester** as their prisoner.)

REGAN: The ungrateful fox! Here he is!

CORNWALL: Tie his withered arms tight!

GLOUCESTER: What do your graces mean?
My good friends, remember you are my guests.
Do me no harm, friends.

CORNWALL: Tie him, I say!

(Servants tie him up.)

REGAN: Tight! Tight! Oh, you filthy traitor!

GLOUCESTER: Merciless lady, I'm *not*!

CORNWALL: Tie him to this chair. What letter
Have you recently received from France?

REGAN: A straight answer, for we know the truth.

GLOUCESTER: I received a vague letter from
A neutral source, not from an enemy.

CORNWALL: Where have you sent the king?

GLOUCESTER: To Dover.

REGAN: Why to Dover?

GLOUCESTER: I couldn't watch your cruel nails
Pluck out his poor old eyes or your sister's
Boarish fangs slash his anointed flesh.

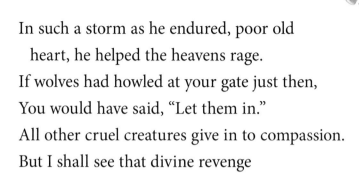

In such a storm as he endured, poor old
   heart, he helped the heavens rage.
If wolves had howled at your gate just then,
You would have said, "Let them in."
All other cruel creatures give in to compassion.
But I shall see that divine revenge
Comes down on such children as you!

CORNWALL: You shall never see it.

(to the servants) You fellows, hold the chair.

I'll set my foot upon those eyes of yours!

(Gloucester is held down in his chair, while Cornwall
blinds one of his eyes with his boot.)

GLOUCESTER: Help! Oh, cruel! Oh, gods!

REGAN: One side will mock the other.

Get the other eye, too!

FIRST SERVANT: Stop, my lord!

I have served you ever since I was a child.

But I've never served you better than I do now

When I tell you to stop!

REGAN: What, you dog!

CORNWALL: You villain!

(He draws his sword and attacks the servant.)

FIRST SERVANT: Right, then, come on! Take your
    chance against an angry man!

(He draws. They fight, and Cornwall is wounded.)

REGAN *(to another servant)*: Give me your sword.
    A peasant dares to stand up like this?

(She runs the servant through from behind.)

FIRST SERVANT: Oh, I am killed! My lord,
    You have one eye left to see some harm
    Come to him! Oh! *(He dies.)*

CORNWALL: In case it should see more,
    I will prevent it.
    (He tears out Gloucester's other eye.)
    Out, you vile piece of jelly!
    Where's your luster now?

GLOUCESTER: All is dark and comfortless.
    Where is my son? Edmund! Call all the
    Sparks of nature to revenge this horrid act!

REGAN: Out, you treacherous villain!
    You are calling on one who hates you.
    It was he who told us of your treasons.

GLOUCESTER: Oh, my follies! Then Edgar
    Was wronged. Kind gods, forgive me for that!

REGAN *(to a servant)*: Go throw him out the gate,

And let him smell his way to Dover.

(to Cornwall) How are you, my lord?

CORNWALL: I am hurt. Follow me, lady.

Turn that eyeless villain out.

And throw his dead servant on the dunghill.

Regan, I'm bleeding badly. This wound is

untimely. Give me your arm.

(**Cornwall** exits, led by **Regan**. **Servants** untie
Gloucester and lead him away. Other **servants** carry
the **dead servant** out.)

SECOND SERVANT: If she has a long life

And in the end dies a natural death,

All women will turn into monsters!

THIRD SERVANT: Let's follow the old duke and

Get the madman to lead him wherever

He wants to go. No one will question

What a madman does.

SECOND SERVANT: You go. I'll fetch some medicine

For his bleeding face. Now, heaven help him!

(**They** exit, in different directions.)

ACT 4

Summary

艾德加帶葛勞塞斯特到多佛時，與
艾德蒙相戀的貢納莉被她丈夫阿爾邦尼公爵尖酸地批評。
一位信差帶來葛勞塞斯特被挖去雙眼的消息，阿爾邦尼誓言
要替葛勞塞斯特報仇。

多佛附近的法軍軍營中，有位紳士告訴肯特，考狄利婭聽見
了父親的處境後，迸發了「神聖的淚水」，但李爾卻因強烈的
羞恥感拒絕與考狄利婭相談。同時，在奧斯華給里根看一
封貢納莉寫給艾德蒙的信後，里根開始懷疑貢納莉對艾德
蒙懷有情意。她同時也告訴奧斯華，若他殺了葛勞塞斯特則
必得拔擢晉升。

李爾王頭上戴著蘆葦編織的王冠並胡言亂語，此舉讓肯特
與葛勞塞斯特相信他真的發瘋了，他們為此感到悲傷，而奧
斯華出現，拔劍衝向葛勞塞斯特。為了保衛父親，艾德加殺
了奧斯華。艾德加在奧斯華口袋中發現貢納莉寫給艾德蒙的
信，並知道她欲殺死她丈夫並嫁給艾德蒙的詭計。

法軍軍營的另一座營帳中，考狄利婭前往探視李爾王，兩
人開心地團聚。同時，法軍和英軍漸漸接近，一場戰役即
將開打。

Scene 1 🎧19

The heath. **Edgar** enters, still disguised as a madman.

EDGAR: It's better like this—openly despised—
Than to be secretly despised but fooled
by flattery.
When things are worst, however,
they can only get better.
But who comes here?

(**Gloucester** enters, led by an **old man**.)

My father, led by a peasant? World, oh, world!
It's hatred of your strange changes that
Helps us accept death.

OLD MAN *(to Gloucester)*: Oh, my good lord,
I've lived on your land for 80 years.

GLOUCESTER: Get away! Good friend, be gone.
Your help can do me no good,
And it may hurt you.

OLD MAN: You cannot see your way.

GLOUCESTER: I have no way, so I need no eyes.
I stumbled when I could see. Very often,
Our misfortunes prove to be assets.

Oh, dear son Edgar, the object of your
Foolish father's anger! If I could only live
To see you by touching you,
I'd say I had eyes again!

OLD MAN *(noticing Edgar)*: It's poor mad Tom, the
beggar.

GLOUCESTER: He must have some sense,
Or else he could not beg.

EDGAR *(aside)*: What's happened to my father?
(aloud) Bless you, master!

GLOUCESTER: Is that the madman?

OLD MAN: Beggar and madman, too, my lord.

GLOUCESTER: Then, please go now, for
Your own safety. I'll ask this man to lead me.

OLD MAN: Alas, sir, he is mad.

GLOUCESTER: It's a sign of the sick times
When madmen lead the blind.
Do as I say. Go!

(**Old man** exits.)

GLOUCESTER: You, there! Hello!

EDGAR: Poor Tom's so cold.

  (aside) I cannot keep this up, but I must!

  (aloud) Bless your sweet eyes, they bleed.

GLOUCESTER: Do you know the way to Dover?

EDGAR: Yes, master.

GLOUCESTER: There is a cliff, whose great height

  Looks fearfully into the pounding sea below.

  Bring me to the edge of it. I'll reward you well.

  From that place I shall need no leading.

EDGAR: Here is my arm. Poor Tom shall lead you.

(**They** exit.)

ACT 4
SCENE
1

Scene ❷

Near the Duke of Albany's palace. **Goneril** and **Edmund** enter, having traveled together from Gloucester's castle.

GONERIL: Welcome, my lord. I'm amazed that
My husband did not meet us on the way.

(**Oswald** enters.)

Where's your master?

OSWALD: Inside, madam. But never was a man
So changed. I told him the army had landed.
He smiled at it. When I told him you were
coming, he said, "So much the worse."
Then I told him of Gloucester's treachery,
And of the loyal service of his son.
He called me an idiot and said I'd got it
The wrong way around!

GONERIL (*to Edmund*): You should go back.
He's too cowardly to take any action.
Go back, Edmund, to my brother-in-law.
Lead his army. I must change roles at home,
And give my husband the sewing to do!
(*pointing to Oswald*) This trusty servant shall be

Our go-between. Soon you might hear—
If you act for your own benefit—
A certain command from your mistress.
(She kisses him.) This kiss, if it dared to speak,
Would raise your spirits up into the air.
Understand me, and farewell.

EDMUND: Yours always, till death!

GONERIL: My dearest Edmund!

(**Edmund** exits.)

Oh, the difference from man to man!
You deserve what a woman has to give,
And I am married to a fool.

OSWALD: Madam, here comes my lord.

(**Oswald** exits. **Albany** enters.)

GONERIL: Wasn't it worth it to come meet me?

ALBANY: Oh, Goneril! You are not worth the dust
    the rude wind blows in your face!
I fear your character. A nature that can deny
Its parent cannot control itself.

GONERIL: Say no more. Your sermon is foolish.

ALBANY: Wisdom and goodness seem vile
To the vile. To the filthy, filth is attractive.

You have driven your gracious father mad.

How could my brother-in-law allow it?

GONERIL: Coward! Everyone pushes you around.

Where's your call to arms? The King of France

Raises his flags in our peaceful land.

The threat of war is all around us—

while you, a moral fool,

Sit still and cry, "Why is he doing this?"

ALBANY: See yourself for what you are—a devil!

Evil is even more horrid in a woman.

GONERIL: You worthless fool!

ALBANY: For shame! Don't act like a monster!
   If I would let my hands follow my emotions,
   I would tear your flesh and bones.
   But your woman's shape protects you.

GONERIL *(sneering)*: You and your manhood!

(A **messenger** enters.)

ALBANY: What news do you have?

MESSENGER: Oh, my good lord,
   The Duke of Cornwall is dead!
   He was slain by his servant as he was
   Putting out the other eye of Gloucester.

ALBANY: Gloucester's eyes!

MESSENGER: A servant, filled with compassion,
   Defended him, raising his sword
   To his great master. The duke, enraged,
   Attacked him, and the servant fell dead—
   But not before giving the duke a mortal
      wound that later took his life.
   (to Goneril) This letter, madam, is from your
      sister.

GONERIL *(aside)*: She being a widow
And my Edmund being with her,
All my dreams for the future might dissolve.
(aloud) I'll read it and answer it.

(**Goneril** exits.)

ALBANY: Where was his son when they
took his eyes?

MESSENGER: On his way here with my lady.

ALBANY: He is not here.

MESSENGER: No, sir. I met him on his way back.

ALBANY: Does he know about the wickedness?

MESSENGER: Yes, my good lord. He was the one
Who informed against his father.
He left the house on purpose so
They would feel free to punish him.

ALBANY: Gloucester, I live to thank you
For the love you showed the king—
And to avenge your eyes!
(to the messenger) Come here, friend.
Tell me all you know.

(**They** exit.)

Scene ❸ 🎧

ACT 4
SCENE 3

The French camp near Dover. **Kent** and a **gentleman** enter.

KENT: Why has the King of France left so soon?

GENTLEMAN: He remembered something he'd forgotten to do in his own kingdom.

KENT: What general has he left in charge?

GENTLEMAN: The Marshal of France.

KENT: Did your letters move Cordelia to any show of grief?

GENTLEMAN: Yes, sir. As she read them,
Tears trickled down her delicate cheek.
Once or twice she gasped "Father!"
As if it pressed upon her heart. She cried,
"Sisters, sisters! Disgrace to all women!
What—in the storm? It's unbelievable!"
Then she shook the holy tears
From her heavenly eyes.

KENT: It is the stars, the stars above us,
That determine our characters! Otherwise,
Parents could not beget such different
children.
Have you spoken with her since?

GENTLEMAN: No.

KENT: Was this before the king returned to France?

GENTLEMAN: No, after.

KENT: Well, the poor distressed Lear is here.
Sometimes, in his clearer moments, he knows
Why we are here, and refuses to see Cordelia.

GENTLEMAN: Why, good sir?

KENT: An overpowering shame pushes him away.
He remembers his own unkindness to her.

GENTLEMAN: Alas, the poor gentleman!

KENT: What have you heard about Albany's and
Cornwall's armies?

GENTLEMAN: They are on the march.

KENT: Well, sir, I'll bring you to our master,
Lear,
And leave you to look after him.
Important business will keep me busy awhile.
When I resume my real name, you won't
Be sorry for your association with me.
Please, come with me now.

(**They** exit.)

Scene 4 🎧 (22)

A tent in the French camp. **Cordelia**, a **doctor**, and **soldiers** enter.

CORDELIA: Alas, it's he. He was seen just now
As mad as the raging sea, singing aloud.
He wore a crown of common weeds.
Find him, and bring him to our sight.

(An **officer** leaves.)

Whoever can cure him
May have all my possessions.

DOCTOR: There is a way, madam. Sleep,
Which he lacks, is how nature cares for us.
There are many herbs whose power
Will close the eye of his anguish.

CORDELIA: May all the remedies of the earth
Be watered with my tears!

(A **messenger** enters.)

MESSENGER: The British army is approaching.

CORDELIA: We know that. We're ready for them.

Oh, dear father! We are fighting for your
   interests. That's why my husband,
      the King of France,
Has pitied my mournful tears.
We are not pushed by ambition, but by
Love, dear love, and our aged father's rights.
May I soon hear and see him!

(**All** exit.)

Scene 5

A room in Gloucester's castle. **Regan** and **Oswald** enter.

REGAN: Have my brother-in-law's troops set out?

OSWALD: Yes, madam.

REGAN: Is he with them?

OSWALD: Madam, after much fuss.
Your sister is the better soldier.

REGAN: Did Lord Edmund speak with your lord
at his home?

OSWALD: No, madam.

REGAN: Why did my sister write to him?

OSWALD: I don't know, lady.

REGAN: Indeed, he has left on a serious matter.
It was stupid to let Gloucester live
After we blinded him. Where he goes,
He turns all hearts against us. Edmund,
I think, has gone to end his father's darkened
life
Out of pity for his misery. He also wants
To discover the strength of the enemy.

OSWALD: I must go after him with this letter.
My lady gave me strict commands about this.

REGAN: Why should she write to Edmund?

Couldn't you give her message by mouth?

Perhaps—I don't know—

I'd really appreciate it—let me open the letter.

OSWALD: Madam, I'd rather—

REGAN: I know she does not love her husband.

I am sure of that. When she was here recently,

She gave loving glances and meaningful looks

To noble Edmund. I know you are close to her.

So listen to this: Edmund and I have talked.

He is more interested in me than in your lady.

You know what I'm saying. Give him this.

(She hands Oswald a letter.)

And when you tell your lady everything

I've told you,

Please advise her to act wisely. So, farewell.

If you do happen to hear of that blind traitor,

There's a promotion for whoever ends his life.

OSWALD: I hope I meet him, madam!

I'll show where my loyalty lies.

REGAN: Farewell.

*(**Both** exit.)*

Scene 6 🎧24

The countryside near Dover. **Gloucester** enters, led by **Edgar**.

GLOUCESTER: How far to the top of that hill?

EDGAR: You're climbing up to it now.

GLOUCESTER: The ground seems level to me.

EDGAR: It's horribly steep. Do you hear the sea?

GLOUCESTER: No, I don't. And I think that
Your voice is changed. You speak more
Clearly than you did before.

EDGAR: You are wrong. I am the same.

GLOUCESTER: No, I think you're better spoken.

EDGAR: Come on, sir. Here's the place. Stand still.
(They're in a field, but Edgar pretends it's a cliff.)
It makes me dizzy to look down!
The fishermen walking on the beach look
As small as mice. I'll look no more,
In case it turns my head. Blurred sight
Might make me topple down headfirst.

GLOUCESTER: Put me where you are standing.

EDGAR: Give me your hand. You are now within
A foot of the extreme edge.

GLOUCESTER: Release my hand. Here, friend,
Is another purse. It holds a valuable jewel.
May good luck help you enjoy it!
Say goodbye, and let me hear you leave.

EDGAR *(pretending to go):* Goodbye, good sir.
(aside) The only reason I toy with his
Despair like this is to cure it.

GLOUCESTER *(kneeling):* Oh, you mighty gods!
I renounce this world and my great pain.
If I could bear it longer, I would.
If Edgar is alive, oh, bless him!
(to Edgar) Now, fellow, farewell!
(He throws himself forward, as if over a cliff.)

EDGAR *(pretending to be far off):* Gone, sir. Farewell.
*(now pretending to be a fisherman at the foot
   of the cliff)* Hello, sir! Friend!
Do you hear me? Speak!
Who are you, sir?

GLOUCESTER: Go away, and let me die.

EDGAR: You have fallen more than the height

Of 10 ships' masts! It's a miracle you're alive!

GLOUCESTER: Have I fallen, or not?

EDGAR: Yes—from the top of this chalky cliff.
Look right up there. Just look up!

GLOUCESTER: Alas, I have no eyes.

EDGAR: Give me your arm. I'll help you up.
How are you? Can you feel your legs?
It is clear that the gods have saved your life.

GLOUCESTER: From now on, I'll bear suffering
Till it decides I've had enough—and then die.

EDGAR: Be patient. But who comes here?

(**Lear** enters, fantastically dressed up with flowers.)

No sane person would dress like that.
What a heartbreaking sight!

LEAR: Look, look, a mouse! Here, this piece
of toasted cheese will catch it. *(He tears off
an imaginary chunk and throws it to the ground.
Then he follows an imaginary arrow in its flight.)*
Oh, well-flown, bird! A bull's eye!
(seeing Edgar) Give the password.

EDGAR: Sweet marjoram.

LEAR: You may pass.

GLOUCESTER: I know you. Are you the king?

LEAR: Yes, every inch a king!

GLOUCESTER: Oh, let me kiss that hand!

LEAR: I must wipe it first. It smells of death.

GLOUCESTER: Oh, what a ruin of a man!
Do you know me?

LEAR: I remember your eyes well enough.
Are you squinting at me?

GLOUCESTER: What, with holes for eyes?

LEAR: Oh, ho, is that your game? No eyes in
your head. Sad for your eyes. But that's
the way of the world, you see.

GLOUCESTER: I see by the feel of things.

LEAR: What, are you mad? A man may see how
The world goes with no eyes. Use your ears.
If you want to weep for my misfortunes,
Take my eyes. I know you well enough.
You are Gloucester. I'll preach to you—listen!

GLOUCESTER: Alas, alas the day!

LEAR: When we're born, we cry that
We have come to this great stage of fools.
(In his madness, he loses his train of thought.)

It would be a good idea to shoe a troop
Of horses with felt. I must try it.
And when I've crept up on these sons-in-law,
Then kill, kill, kill, kill!

(A **gentleman** enters, with **attendants**.)

GENTLEMAN: Oh, here he is. Take hold of him.

LEAR: I am a king. Do you realize that?

GENTLEMAN: You are a royal one. We obey you.

LEAR: Then there's still hope. Come, if you
want it, you'll have to run for it!

(**He** runs off. The **attendants** run after him.)

GENTLEMAN: A pitiful sight even for the lowest
wretch! When it's a king, it's beyond words!

EDGAR: Have you heard of a coming battle?

GENTLEMAN: Of course. Everyone has.

EDGAR: How close is the other army?

GENTLEMAN: Very near, and approaching fast.

EDGAR: Thank you, sir. That's all.

(**Gentleman** exits.)

GLOUCESTER: Now, good sir, who are you?

EDGAR: A very poor man, broken by misfortune.
   Give me your hand. I'll lead you to shelter.

GLOUCESTER: Hearty thanks.

(**Oswald** enters, and sees Gloucester.)

OSWALD: A man with a price on his head! Happy
   day! Your eyeless head will make my fortune!
   (He draws his sword.) You unhappy old traitor,
   The sword is out that will destroy you.

GLOUCESTER *(ready to die):* Let your friendly hand
   Be strong enough to do it.

(**Edgar** steps forward to defend his father.)

OSWALD: You bold peasant, how dare you
   Defend an outlawed traitor? Let go his arm.

EDGAR: I'll not let go, sir, without a better reason.

OSWALD: Let go, wretch, or you'll die!

EDGAR: If I could have been cheated out
   Of my life, I'd have lost it weeks ago.
   Come on! I'm not afraid of your sword!

(They fight, and Edgar wounds him. Oswald falls down.)

OSWALD: Wretch, you have killed me! Villain,
   Take my purse. If you ever hope to prosper,

Bury my body. Give the letter I'm carrying
To Edmund, Earl of Gloucester.
Find him on the English side.
Oh, untimely death! *(He dies.)*

EDGAR: I know you well. A true villain,
Willing to serve the vices of your mistress.

GLOUCESTER: What—is he dead?

EDGAR: Sit down, good sir, and rest.
Let's see what's in these pockets.
The letter he spoke of might be useful.
(He finds the letter and breaks the wax seal.)
I beg your pardon, gentle wax. Don't say This is
bad manners. To know what's in our Enemies'
minds, we'd rip their hearts!
It's more lawful to rip open their letters.
*(He reads.) Remember our mutual vows. You'll
have many chances to kill him. If he returns*

*the winner, we shall have accomplished
nothing. Then I would be his prisoner, and
his bed my jail. From this fate, please save
me, and assure yourself of my love.*

Your wife (or so I wish),

And your loving servant,

Goneril

Oh, how unlimited is woman's evil!
A plot to kill her virtuous husband,
And my brother to replace him!
(to Oswald) I'll show this wicked letter
To the duke. It's good that I can tell him
Of your death and your wicked business.

(**Edgar** exits, dragging **Oswald's body**.)

GLOUCESTER: The king is mad. How stubborn
My mind is, that I remain sane enough
To know my huge sorrows! Better I were mad
And my thoughts cut off from my griefs.

(Drums are heard from far off.)

EDGAR: Come now. I'll leave you with a friend.

(**Both** exit.)

Scene 7

A tent in the French camp. **Lear** is on a bed, asleep. Music plays. **Doctor**, **gentleman**, and **others** are attending Lear. **Cordelia** and **Kent** enter.

CORDELIA: Oh, good Kent! How could I ever
Repay you for your goodness?

KENT: To be appreciated, lady, is to be overpaid.

CORDELIA: Change your clothes. Those garments
Are reminders of those bad times.

KENT: Madam, to be recognized now
Goes against my plans. I ask you the favor
Of not knowing me till I think
  the time is right.

CORDELIA: So be it, my good lord.
(to the doctor) How is the king?

DOCTOR: Madam, he's still sleeping. Would you
Allow us to wake him? He has slept long.

CORDELIA: Do as you think best.

DOCTOR: Be here, madam, when we wake him.
I do not doubt that he'll be normal.

CORDELIA: Very well. *(to Lear)* Oh, dear father!

ACT **4**
SCENE
7

May my lips bring healing, and let this kiss
Repair those violent harms that my two sisters
Have done to you! *(She kisses his forehead.)*

KENT: Kind and dear princess!

CORDELIA: Even if you had not been their father,
Your white hair should have merited pity.
Was this a face to fight against the storm?
To stand against the fearful thunder?
To stay in the midst of the awful lightning?
To be up at night—poor lost soul—
With this thin head-covering? My enemy's dog,
Even if he had bit me, would have had a place

In front of my fire that night. Alas, alas!
It's a wonder that your life and your sanity
Didn't end together. He is waking. Talk to him.

DOCTOR: Madam, you do so. It's best.

CORDELIA *(to Lear)*: How is my royal lord?

LEAR: You do me wrong to take me
Out of the grave. You are a soul in bliss,
But I am suffering, tied to a wheel of fire.
My own tears scald me like molten lead.

CORDELIA: Sir, do you know me?

LEAR: You are a spirit, I know. When did you die?

CORDELIA *(to the doctor)*: He is still confused.

DOCTOR: He's barely awake.

LEAR: Where have I been? Where am I?

CORDELIA: Give me your blessing, sir.

(Lear sees her, and then falls at her feet.)

No, sir, you must not kneel!

LEAR: Please do not mock me.
I am a very foolish old man, over 80 years old.
And, truthfully, I fear I'm not in my right
mind.

I think I should know you, and know this
man, too.
Yet I am doubtful. I do not even remember
Where I slept last night. Do not laugh at me.
I think this lady is my child Cordelia.

CORDELIA: And so I am. I am.

LEAR: Are your tears wet? Yes, indeed. Don't cry.
If you have poison for me, I will drink it. I
Know you do not love me. Your sisters have,
As I remember, done me wrong:
You have some cause. They have not.

CORDELIA: *(weeping):* No cause, no cause.

DOCTOR: Take comfort, madam. The madness,
You see, is calmed in him. Yet it is dangerous
To fill the gaps in his memory.
Don't trouble him any more until he's calmer.

CORDELIA: Would your highness like to walk?

LEAR: You must be patient with me. Please now,
forget and forgive. I am old and foolish.

(**Lear, Cordelia, doctor**, and **attendants** exit.)

GENTLEMAN: Was Cornwall really killed like that?

KENT: Most certainly, sir.

GENTLEMAN: Who now commands his people?

KENT: The illegitimate son of Gloucester, it's said.

GENTLEMAN: They say Edgar, his banished son, is with the Earl of Kent in Germany.

KENT: The stories change. We must prepare. The armies of the kingdom approach quickly.

GENTLEMAN: The battle is likely to be bloody. Farewell, sir.

(**Gentleman** exits.)

KENT: My life depends on this day's battle.

(**Kent** exits.)

ACT 5

Summary

當貢納莉和里根不斷爭相索取艾德蒙的愛時，李爾和考狄利婭被逮捕。艾德蒙和阿爾邦尼爭辯舉辦審判的地點。阿爾邦尼眼見里根與艾德蒙為夥，感到非常憤怒。里根抱怨身體不適，阿爾邦尼則提出與艾德蒙決鬥。艾德加上前表明他將代替葛勞塞斯特與艾德蒙決鬥，艾德蒙決鬥後身負重傷。阿爾邦尼出其不意地拿出貢納莉寫給艾德蒙的書信，以此作為她背叛自己的有力證據。當她因絕望而惱羞離去，艾德蒙承認他的邪惡計謀，而艾德加則向阿爾邦尼透漏他的真實身分。

接著，當艾德加告訴阿爾邦尼被驅逐出境的肯特所扮演的角色後，傳來貢納莉毒害里根後自我了斷的消息。此時艾德蒙也透露他已下令處死李爾王與考狄利婭。一名軍官跑去傳達暫緩行刑的消息，李爾王進門，懷中抱著死去的考狄利婭。李爾王悲戚不已，而阿爾邦尼、肯特和艾德加則感嘆李爾王為「沉淪的高貴之人」。最後，李爾王因心碎而死，阿爾邦尼宣布「王國的重擔」將由肯特和艾德加共同肩負。

Scene ❶ 🎧 26

The camp of the British forces near Dover. **Edmund**, **Regan**, **officers**, **soldiers**, and **others** enter.

REGAN: Now, sweet lord,

Tell me, honestly, do you not love my sister?

EDMUND: In an honorable way.

REGAN: Have you never been intimate with her?

EDMUND: No, by my honor, madam.

REGAN: I shall never tolerate her, my lord.

Do not be familiar with her.

EDMUND: Don't worry.

(A drum sounds.)

Here she is, with her husband!

(**Albany**, **Goneril**, and **soldiers** enter.)

GONERIL *(aside)*: I'd rather lose the battle than

Have my sister come between him and me.

ALBANY *(bowing to Regan)*: Greetings, dear sister.

(to Edmund) Sir, I heard this:

The king has gone to his daughter, along with

Others who were forced to leave as a result

Of our harsh rule. I never liked this business.

It concerns us only because France invades us.

REGAN: Why do you bother to say this?

GONERILL: Unite against the enemy.

These family matters are not the question here.

ALBANY: Let's ask the experts how to proceed.

EDMUND: We shall meet you soon in your tent.

(Before anyone can leave, **Edgar** enters, disguised.)

EDGAR *(to Albany)*: May I have a word with you?

ALBANY *(to the others)*: I'll catch up with you.

(**All** but Albany and Edgar exit.)

(to Edgar) Speak.

EDGAR: Before the battle, open this letter.

If you win, let the trumpet sound.

Humble though I seem, I can produce

A champion who will prove what is said here.

If you lose, you won't care about anything,

And there all matters will end. Good luck!

ALBANY: Stay till I have read the letter.

EDGAR: I was forbidden to do so.

At the right time, just let the trumpets sound,

And I'll appear again.

ALBANY: Farewell, then. I'll read your letter.

(**Edgar** exits. **Edmund** enters again.)

EDMUND: The enemy's in view.

Bring up your troops. Act quickly now.

ALBANY: We will do our best.

(**Albany** exits.)

EDMUND: I have sworn my love to both

These sisters. Each is suspicious of the other.

Which of them shall I take? Both? One?

Or neither? Neither can be enjoyed

If both remain alive. To take the widow

Would make her sister Goneril very angry.

But with Goneril's husband alive,

I can hardly accomplish my plan.

So for now we'll use him for the battle.

When it's over, she who wants to be rid of

Him can decide. As for the mercy

He wants to show Lear and Cordelia,

Once the battle is done and we have them,

They shall never see his pardon. My interests

Are best served by action, not thought.

(**Edmund** exits.)

ACT**5**
SCENE
1

Scene 2

A field between the two camps. **Lear** and **Cordelia** cross the stage with some of their troops, and exit. Then **Edgar** and **Gloucester** enter.

EDGAR: Good sir, rest under this tree.

Pray that the right side wins. If I return,

I'll bring you comforting news.

GLOUCESTER: May grace go with you, sir!

(**Edgar** exits. The sounds of war grow louder. A retreat is sounded. **Edgar** enters again, dismayed.).

EDGAR: Let's go, old man! King Lear has lost.

He and his daughter have been captured.

Give me your hand. Come on!

(**They** exit.)

Scene ❸ 🎧 28

The British camp near Dover. **Edmund** enters, with **Lear** and **Cordelia** as prisoners. Soldiers guard them.

EDMUND: Guard them well until we find out
What our leaders want to do with them.

CORDELIA *(to Lear)*: We are not the first
To suffer the worst from good intentions.

LEAR: Let's be off to prison. We two, alone,
Will sing like birds in a cage. When you ask
A blessing of me, I'll kneel down and beg
Your forgiveness. So we'll live, and pray,
And sing, and tell old stories, and laugh
At the courtiers in their fancy clothes.

ACT**5**
SCENE
3

EDMUND: Take them away.

LEAR: The gods themselves bless such sacrifices
As yours, Cordelia. *(She cries.)* Don't cry.
Nothing can separate us now. Wipe your eyes.
They'll rot before they'll make us weep. Come!

(**Lear** and **Cordelia** exit, guarded.)

EDMUND *(to an officer)*: Come here, captain.
Take this note. Follow them to prison.
Obey these instructions and I'll reward you.

Know this: Men must take advantage

Of their opportunities. A soldier cannot be

Tenderhearted. Either say you'll do it,

Or prosper by some other means.

CAPTAIN: I can't pull a cart like a horse.

If it's man's work, I'll do it.

(**He** exits. Trumpets sound. **Albany**, **Goneril**, **Regan**, **officers**, and **attendants** enter.)

ALBANY *(to Edmund)*: I require the captives

taken in today's battle—

To do with them what they deserve.

EDMUND: Sir, I thought it best to keep them

Away from here under guard. The king's

Age and title might sway the emotions

Of the common people—and turn our own

Soldiers against us. Tomorrow, or later,

Would be a better time to hold their trial.

ALBANY: Sir, hold on. I see you as a subject

In this war—not as an equal.

REGAN *(to Albany)*: He led our troops

And acted on my authority. That's enough

To give him rank as your equal.

GONERIL: Not so fast. He merits high rank
   In his own right rather than with your help.

REGAN: By acting in my name, on my authority,
   He equals the best.

GONERIL: It would be so only if he married you.

REGAN: Jesters often prove to be prophets.

GONERIL *(sarcastically)*: Well, well, well.

REGAN: Lady, I am not well. Otherwise,
   I'd give you a piece of my mind.
   (to Edmund) General, take my soldiers, my
      prisoners,
   My inheritance. Do what you want with them,
   And with me. May the world witness that
   I hereby create you my lord and master.

ACT 5
SCENE 3

GONERIL: Do you plan to marry him?

ALBANY *(to Goneril, angrily)*: It's not up to you!

EDMUND: Nor to you, lord.

ALBANY: Indeed it is!

REGAN *(to Edmund)*: Let the drum sound
   And proclaim that what is mine, is yours.

ALBANY: Hold on. Listen to reason! Edmund,
I arrest you for treason, and as your accomplice
(pointing to Goneril), this gilded serpent!

GONERIL: Such drama!

ALBANY: You are armed, Edmund.
Let the trumpet sound. If no one comes to
Prove in combat your many treasons,
I'll do it myself! There is my challenge!
(He throws down a glove.)

REGAN: Sick, oh, I'm sick!

GONERIL *(aside)*: If not, I'll never trust poison.

EDMUND *(throwing down a glove)*: My response!
He who calls me a traitor lies like a villain!
Whoever dares to approach, I will defend
My honor against him, you, or anyone else!

ALBANY *(calling)*: A herald, there!

REGAN *(about to fall)*: My sickness grows worse.

ALBANY: She is not well. Take her to my tent.

(**Regan** exits, helped by **officers**. A **herald** enters.)

Come here, herald. Sound the trumpet, and
read this. *(He hands him Edmund's challenge.)*

(Herald sounds the trumpet.)

120

HERALD *(reading)*: *If any man of rank or distinction in the army says that Edmund, Earl of Gloucester, is a traitor, let him appear by the third sound of the trumpet. He will defend himself boldly.*

(Trumpet sounds three times, with pauses in between. Then **Edgar** comes forth, announced by more trumpeting.)

HERALD: Who are you to answer the call?

EDGAR: My name is not on record.
Treason has destroyed it. Yet I am as noble
As the man I come to fight.

ALBANY: Who is that man?

EDGAR: Who fights for Edmund, Earl of
Gloucester?

EDMUND *(stepping forward)*: He himself.
What have you to say to him?

EDGAR: Draw your sword. Here is mine!
You are a traitor, false to your gods,
Your brother, and your father. Deny it,
And this sword, this arm, and my best spirits
Are determined to prove that you lie!

EDMUND: According to the rules of knighthood,

I could delay this fight. But I refuse to do this.

I toss your accusations of treason back at you,

Along with the hateful charge of lying.

This sword of mine will thrust them home,

Where they shall rest forever. Trumpets, speak!

(Trumpets sound. Edmund and Edgar fight. Edmund falls, badly wounded.)

ALBANY: Save him, save him!

GONERIL: This is a trick, Edmund.

By the code of arms, you were not obliged

To fight an unknown enemy.

You are not defeated, but cheated and beguiled.

ALBANY: Shut your mouth, woman, or I'll shut it

With this paper! *(It is Goneril's letter to Edmund,*

which Edgar had found on Oswald in

Act 4, Scene 6.)

(to Edgar) Hold your sword, sir.

(to Goneril) You are too wicked for words!

I suspect you know what this is.

(Edmund takes the letter.)

GONERIL: What if I do? I am the queen.

The law belongs to me, not you.

Who can prosecute me for it?

ALBANY: Monster! Do you know this letter?

GONERIL: Don't ask me what I know.

(**Goneril** exits, upset.)

ALBANY *(to an officer)*: Go after her. She's

desperate. Take care of her. *(Officer leaves.)*

EDMUND *(to Albany)*: What you have charged

Me with, I have done—and more,

much more.

Time will reveal all. It's over now, and so am I.

(to Edgar) But who are you, who have this
Victory on me? If you are a noble man,
I forgive you.

EDGAR: I am no less royal than you are, Edmund.
My name is Edgar, and I am your father's son.
The gods are just. They use the vices we enjoy
As the means to punish us. Conceiving you
Cost him his eyes.

EDMUND: You've said right. It's true.

ALBANY *(to Edgar)***:** I thought your very walk
Suggested a royal nobility. I welcome you.
Let sorrow split my heart if I ever
Hated you or your father!

EDGAR: Worthy prince, I know that.

ALBANY: Where have you been hiding?
How did you know your father's miseries?

EDGAR: By nursing them, my lord.
Listen to a brief tale. To escape the threat
Of death that was upon me, I dressed in rags
And behaved like a madman. In this clothing
I met my father with his bleeding eye sockets
After he'd been blinded. I became his guide,
Begged for him, saved him from despair.

I never revealed myself to him until
Half an hour ago, when I was in armor.
I asked his blessing and told him of my
    pilgrimage
From first to last. His injured heart, torn
Between joy and grief, burst with happiness.

EDMUND: This speech of yours has touched me,
And it may do some good. Go on.
You look as if you have more to say.

EDGAR: While I was bawling out my grief
A man came by. When he recognized me,
He wrapped his strong arms around my neck
And cried out as if he'd burst the heavens.
Then he embraced my father, and told him
The most pitiful tale of Lear and himself
That anyone ever heard. As he told it,
His grief grew stronger, and his hold on life
Began to slip. Then the trumpets sounded,
    and I left him, unconscious.

ALBANY: But who was this?

EDGAR: Kent, sir—the banished Kent.
In disguise he followed the king who had
Banished him, serving him better
    than any slave.

(A **gentleman** enters, holding a bloody knife.)

GENTLEMAN: Help, help! Oh, help!

EDGAR: What does that bloody knife mean?

GENTLEMAN: It's warm . . . it's steaming . . .
It came from the heart of . . . Oh! She's dead!

ALBANY: Who's dead? Speak, man.

GENTLEMAN: Your lady, sir, your wife. And she
Has poisoned her sister. She has confessed it.

EDMUND: I was engaged to both of them!
All three of us will be united soon.

EDGAR: Here comes Kent.

ALBANY: Bring in the bodies, alive or dead.
The judgment of the heavens, which we fear,
has no pity on us.

(The **gentleman** leaves. **Kent** enters.)

KENT: I have come to bid my king and master
An everlasting good night. Is he not here?

ALBANY: A serious oversight! Speak, Edmund,
Where's the king? And where's Cordelia?

(The bodies of **Goneril** and **Regan** are brought in.)

Do you see this, Kent?

KENT: Alas! What happened?

EDMUND: So Edmund was indeed loved!
One poisoned the other for my sake,
And then killed herself.

ALBANY: Indeed so. Cover their faces.

EDMUND: I pant for life. I want to do some good,
In spite of my own nature. Go quickly
To the castle! I've given orders there for the
Deaths of Lear and Cordelia. Make haste.
Get there in time.

ALBANY: Run, run! Oh, run!

EDGAR: To whom, my lord? Who is in charge?
Send your token, ordering a reprieve.

EDMUND: Good thinking. Take my sword.
Give it to the captain.

EDGAR *(giving Edmund's sword to an officer)*: Hurry!
On your life!

(The **officer** runs off.)

EDMUND *(to Albany)*: He has orders from
Your wife and me to hang Cordelia in the
Prison and say her despair led to her suicide.

ACT 5
SCENE
3

127

ALBANY: May the gods protect her!

(to servants) Take him away for the moment.

(**Edmund** is carried off. **Lear** enters again, with **Cordelia** dead in his arms.)

LEAR: Howl, howl, howl, howl! Oh, you are men
Of stone! She's gone forever!

KENT *(kneeling before Lear)*: Oh, my good master!

LEAR: Go away!

EDGAR: It is the noble Kent, your friend.

LEAR: A plague upon you! Murderers, traitors!

I might have saved her.

Now she's gone forever! Cordelia, Cordelia!

Stay awhile!

(He puts his ear to her lips.) What's that you say?

Her voice was ever soft, gentle, and

Low—an excellent thing in woman.

I killed the wretch who was hanging you!

OFFICER: It's true, my lords. He did.

LEAR: Didn't I, man?

(seeing Kent) Who are you? Aren't you Kent?

ACT 5
SCENE
3

KENT: The same. Your servant, Kent.

Where is your servant Caius?

LEAR *(recognizing the name Kent used when disguised)***:**

He's a good fellow, I can tell you that!

He'll fight, and quickly, too.

(sadly) He's dead and decayed.

KENT: No, my good lord. I am the very man

Who has followed in your sad steps

From the beginning of your declining fortunes.

LEAR *(not understanding)***:** You are welcome here.

KENT: All is dreary, dark, and deadly. Your
    Eldest daughters have killed themselves in
      hopeless desperation.

LEAR *(still not understanding)*: Yes, I think so.

ALBANY: He doesn't know what he is saying.
    It's no use to talk to him.

EDGAR: No use at all.

(An **officer** enters.)

OFFICER: Edmund is dead, my lord.

ALBANY: That's of little importance here.
    Lords and nobles, know what I intend to do.
    We shall comfort this noble ruin of mankind
    As best we can. As for us, we will resign
    And turn our power over to this old majesty
    For the remainder of his life.
    (to Edgar and Kent) As for you,
    You resume your honorable places,
    With such additional titles as your noble deeds
    Have more than earned. All friends shall
    Be rewarded for their loyalty, and all foes
    Punished as they deserve. Oh, look, look!

LEAR: My poor child is hanged! No, no, no life!
Why should a dog, a horse, a rat, have life,
And you no breath at all? You'll come no more,
Never, never, never, never, never!
(He struggles with his collar.) Please,
Undo this button. Thank you, sir.
Do you see this? Look at her! Look! Her lips!
Look there, look there!
(Overcome by grief, he dies.)

EDGAR: He's fainted! *(shaking Lear)* My lord!

KENT: Break, heart. I beg you, break!

EDGAR *(still shaking Lear)***:** Wake up, my lord!

KENT: Don't trouble his departing spirit.
Let him go! Only an enemy would make
Him suffer any longer in this rough world.

ALBANY: Bear them away. General mourning
Is our present concern.
(to Kent and Edgar) Friends, you two shall bear
the burden of this kingdom.

EDGAR: We must get through this sad time.
The oldest have suffered most. We young
Shall never see so much, nor live so long.

(The bodies are taken away in a slow march.)

中文翻譯·

背景 —————————————————————— 英文內文 P. 004

李爾王是個固執又驕傲的老頭，他決定要將王國分給三個女兒，並將其中最大的領土留給最愛他的那位。可惜他分辨不出屈意奉承與真誠的愛，於是將他的么女誠實的考狄利婭驅逐出境。他將王國分給貢納莉與里根，然後這兩個「貼了金箔的毒蛇」就不再虛情假意了，她們聯手掠奪了他所有的財產，不再假裝自己是孝順的女兒。李爾漸漸地發瘋了，但是在他最低潮的時刻，他開始認識自己的這個血肉之軀。

和李爾一樣，葛勞塞斯特也看不清親生孩子——他的私生子艾德蒙的邪惡。只有在他被敵人弄瞎，又在絕望之餘意圖自盡卻被他的另一個兒子艾德加所救之後，他才看清事實的真相。邪惡殘害了李爾與葛勞塞斯特——但是他們的身體創傷都有正面的結果，那就是精神上的重生。

人物介紹 ──────────────── P. 005

李爾：不列顛國王

法王：考狄利婭的追求者之一

貢納莉：李爾的長女

阿爾邦尼公爵：貢納莉的丈夫

里根：李爾的次女

康沃爾公爵：里根的丈夫

考狄利婭：李爾的么女

勃艮第公爵：考狄利婭的追求者之一

肯特伯爵：李爾的忠誠朝臣

葛勞塞斯特伯爵：李爾的忠誠朝臣

艾德加：葛勞塞斯特的長子，後來偽裝成衣衫襤褸的乞丐「窮酸湯姆」

艾德蒙：葛勞塞斯特的次子，私生子

奧斯華：貢納莉的管家

庫朗：葛勞塞斯特的僕人

老人：葛勞塞斯特的佃戶

醫生

傻子：李爾的弄臣

騎士們、軍官們、信差們、士兵們、僕人們與侍從們

（英格蘭。在李爾王宮殿的一個大廳；肯特、葛勞塞斯特與艾德蒙上。）

肯特：我認為國王愛阿爾邦尼公爵，更甚於他愛康沃爾公爵。

葛勞塞斯特：如今他已分割了他的王國，他最重視哪位公爵仍是未定之天。兩位公爵是如此均等，未有彼此相爭之情事。

肯特（指著艾德蒙）：這不是令郎嗎，閣下？

葛勞塞斯特：我是他的父親，先生，卻經常羞於承認與他的關係，如今已是麻木而毫無感覺。

肯特：我難以想見這理由何在。

葛勞塞斯特：先生，這年輕人的母親可以想見！她尚未結婚與丈夫同床共枕，即有孕而生了一個兒子來養育。你是否看出問題何在？

肯特：即使有此問題又何妨，結果是如此地美好啊！

葛勞塞斯特：但是我有個婚生子，較於這個兒子更為年長，唯我並未因此而偏愛他。你認識這位高貴的紳士嗎，艾德蒙？

艾德蒙：不認識，閣下。

葛勞塞斯特（正式介紹他）：他是肯特伯爵，也是我可敬的好友。

艾德蒙：聽候你的差遣，父親。

（號角聲響起。）

葛勞塞斯特：國王來了。

（一名僕人上，手裡捧著王冠，李爾王、康沃爾公爵、阿爾邦尼公爵、貢納莉、里根、考狄利婭與侍從們尾隨而上。）

李爾：將法王和勃艮第公爵找來，葛勞塞斯特。

葛勞塞斯特：好的，陛下。

（葛勞塞斯特與艾德蒙下。）

李爾：此時也該透露我們的計畫了，將那份地圖遞給我。（僕人們送上一份地圖。）朕已將王國一分為三，朕希望能擺脫煩惱而頤養天年，將此重任交予年輕的一輩擔負，讓朕得以無憂無慮地等待生命終了。告訴我，我的女兒們，在你們當中是誰最愛朕？朕欲將最大的一份交予最孝順朕的女兒。貢納莉，我的長女，你先說。

貢納莉：陛下，我對你的愛超乎我所能言喻，你比雙眼所能見、空間所能容和自由所能及更加地珍貴，與生命同等重要。

考狄利婭（竊語）：考狄利婭應如何回答？只消有愛即可，保持緘默……

李爾（指著地圖上貢納莉的嫁妝）：由此地至此地，遍佈茂密的森林、肥沃的平原和魚獲豐沛的河流，朕交予你永世統治。（轉向里根）朕的次女怎麼說？說吧。

里根：除了在你的父愛中得到的快樂，我別無他求。

考狄利婭（竊語）：可憐的考狄莉婭啊！唯事實並不然，因我確信我的愛已超乎我所能言喻。

李爾：朕將這三分之一的王國，交予你和你的繼承人，朕給你的地幅、價值和快樂皆不亞於貢納莉。（轉向考狄利婭：）朕同樣疼愛的么女啊——你要怎麼說才能得到比兩位姊姊更珍貴的三分之一王國？說吧。

考狄利婭：我無話可說，陛下。

李爾：無話可說！

考狄利婭：無話可說。

李爾：無話可說即無有所得。再說一次。

考狄利婭：我無法表達內心的情感。我愛陛下如一般女兒應盡孝道，既不多，亦不少。

李爾：你何出此言，考狄利婭？

考狄利婭：我的好陛下，你生養我、教導我、愛我，我盡了義務回報這一切，我服從你、愛你並無比尊崇你。倘若我的兩位姊姊說她們將全部的愛獻給你，她們又何以嫁人從夫？但願在我結婚之後，我的丈夫能擁有我一半的愛、關懷和照顧。

李爾：這番話可是你的肺腑之言？

考狄利婭：是的，我的好陛下。

李爾：才這麼年輕就如此薄情嗎？

考狄利婭：我年紀雖輕卻誠實無欺，陛下。

李爾：那就以你的誠實當你的嫁妝吧！憑著神聖的陽光，憑著
主宰我們生命的繁星，朕在此與你斷絕關係！你如今已失
去朕的關愛和朕這個父親，永遠離開此地吧，與朕再無關
係的女兒。

肯特：陛下——

李爾：安靜，肯特！朕最是疼愛考狄利婭，一心以為她會陪朕
共度遲暮之年。去吧，遠離朕的視線！朕唯有進了墳墓才能
得到平靜，因朕就此剝奪對她的父愛。康沃爾與阿爾邦尼，
在朕兩個女兒的嫁妝之外，這第三份也分給你們：就讓驕
傲，亦即她所謂的誠實，迎娶她為妻吧！朕在此將權力、威
嚴和伴隨王位而來的所有榮耀風光，悉數移交給你們。朕
將每月輪流與你們同住，保留一百名騎士，費用由你們支
付。朕只留王位頭銜和國王應有的榮耀，政策、賦稅和瑣務
皆交由你們處理，兩位親愛的半子。為確認此一決定，這王
冠交由你倆共同保管。

（僕人將王冠交給兩位公爵。）

肯特：李爾王陛下，我一向擁戴你為國王、愛你如我的父親
——當李爾失去理智之際，肯特不得不無禮。你在做什麼，
老頭？在國王開始做起蠢事之時，為保名譽就得直言勸諫。
保住你的王國，對你倉促的決定再行三思。我願以性命為
賭注——你的么女並非愛你最少，言語中未有奉承恭維者
亦非無情無義。

李爾：肯特，莫再多言，否則你性命難保！

肯特：為保陛下之安全，我毫不懼怕失去我的性命。

李爾：遠離朕的視線！

肯特：放亮你的眼睛，李爾，讓我——一如往常地——為了陛下而睜大雙眼。

李爾：聽好了，叛徒！既然你意圖使朕違背誓言——於此朕未有過前例——仔細聽好！朕給你五日期限，處理好你在這世間的繁務。到了第六天就轉過你可恨的身子離開朕的王國；倘若你到第十天仍逗留於此地——那一刻即為你的死期。你走吧！朕對天起誓，君無戲言！

肯特：再會了，國王陛下。倘若此為你所願，那我去別處尋找自由。（**對考狄利婭：**）願眾神保護你，丫頭。你的想法沒錯，你的所言亦為真！（**對里根與貢納莉：**）但願你倆天花亂墜的說詞，皆能一一化為實踐。

（肯特下。號角聲宣告葛勞塞斯特、法蘭斯王、勃艮第公爵與他們的侍從們上場。）

李爾：勃艮第公爵閣下，朕先問你，你一直在追求小女，你要求的嫁妝至少為何，否則你就會放棄向小女求愛？

勃艮第：最尊貴的國王陛下，我的要求莫過於你已應許的。

李爾：當朕疼愛她之時，朕珍視她勝過其他，而如今她已然貶值；以她目前的處境，朕對她甚是不悅，所以毫無所賜，沒有嫁妝。倘若你還要她，就帶她走吧。

勃艮第（惱怒）：我無言以對。

李爾：你要帶她走或是離開她？

勃艮第：原諒我，陛下，在如此的條件下我無法決定。

李爾：那就離開她吧，閣下，因朕已將她的價值告知予你。（**對法王：**）至於你，偉大的國王，朕不能讓朕憎恨的女兒委身於你，如此可能損及你與朕的友誼，所以朕懇請你轉而追求更值得的對象。

法王：此事甚為蹊蹺！你如此疼愛她，她是你晚年的慰藉；難道她突然做了極其可怕之事，使你對她的疼愛盡失？你對她的疼愛想必是虛假的，否則就是她對你實在是大不敬；我難以置信她會做出此等劣行。

考狄利婭：請求陛下公告世人，我失去你的仁慈和寵愛並非起因於罪行、殺人或邪惡之事，而是因為我不懂得討你歡心，不會巧言奉承，雖然我也很慶幸自己不會如此。

法王：果真如此嗎？羞怯的天性經常使得內心的感情無法表達？勃艮第公爵閣下，你有何話要對這位小姐說明？當愛情混雜著偏離主題的顧慮之時，愛情就不是愛情了。你願意娶她嗎？她唯一的嫁妝就是她自己。

勃艮第（對李爾）：尊貴的陛下，賜與你所許諾的嫁妝吧，我會即刻娶考狄利婭為妻。

李爾：朕毫無所賜，朕已立下誓言。

勃艮第（對考狄利婭）：那就抱歉了，你在失去父親的同時也失去了丈夫。

考狄利婭：但願勃艮第公爵平安！既然他如此愛面子和財富，我也不願委身於他為妻。

法王：最美麗的考狄利婭，我在此請求你將自身和你的美德交予我！倘若這是合乎律法，我將接受你這被摒棄之人。眾神！眾神啊！他們的冷漠忽視竟使我的愛更為熾烈，真令人費解！就讓你身無分文的女兒成為我的王后。道聲再見吧，考狄利婭，雖然他們待你無情，但是你在此地失去的將在別處得到更多。

李爾：帶她走吧，法王，朕沒有這個女兒，也不想再見到她這張臉了。去吧，朕不會給她仁慈、疼愛或祝福。走吧，尊貴的勃艮第。

（李爾、勃艮第、康沃爾、阿爾邦尼、葛勞塞斯特與侍從們下。）

法王：向你的兩位姊姊道別吧。

考狄利婭：我父親的兩位掌上明珠，我要含淚離開你們了。我知道你們的真實面貌，但是身為小妹，我不想細數你們的缺失。請你們如方才所言一般照顧好父王，唯我寧可他能有更好的去處。

貢納莉：盡力取悅你的丈夫吧，他是命運施捨給你的，你有如此歸宿已是大幸。

考狄利婭：時間會揭露欺瞞所掩蓋的真相，藏起自身缺陷之人終將蒙羞。但願你從此平步青雲！

法王：走吧，我美麗的考狄利婭。

（法王與考狄利婭下。）

貢納莉：妹妹，我們有共同的利益要詳加商議，我們的父王今晚就要離開。

里根：你先帶他走，下個月再讓他來與我們同住。

貢納莉：你也看到他於遲暮之年有多大的改變！他一向最寵愛我們的小妹，而今他已將她驅逐出境，他的識人不清已是可見一斑。

里根：那是因為他已年邁，但是話又說回來，他一向是欠缺自制力。

貢納莉：他即便是年輕時也是脾氣暴躁，所以我們如今不僅
會看到他終身未變的老毛病——也會見識到他因年老病弱
而招致的新缺失。

里根：難怪我們能預見他放逐肯特的一時衝動。

貢納莉：他向法王告別時也失了禮數！好吧，我們這就從長計
議。倘若父王繼續如此輕率地行使他的權威，他將會成為
我們的燙手山芋。

里根：我們必須想辦法——儘快採取行動！

（貢納莉與里根下。）

（葛勞塞斯特伯爵的城堡大廳；艾德蒙上，手裡拿著一封信。）

艾德蒙（自言自語）：為何社會要限制我的權利，只因我較我的兄長年幼十二或十四個月？又為何――只因我的父親並未迎娶我的母親――我就要被視為矮人一截？我和任何已婚婦女所生之子同樣地聰明和英俊。合法婚生子艾德加，我一定要奪取你的繼承權！我們的父親愛我如同他愛你一般。（揮舞信件。）倘若這封信奏效，我的計畫就成功了，私生子艾德蒙將擊敗婚生子艾德加！我將青雲直上！

（他的父親葛勞塞斯特伯爵上。）

葛勞塞斯特：肯特竟如此被驅逐出境！而法王也負氣離去！國王放棄了他的大權，他做的這一切只是一時衝動！（注意到他的兒子。）艾德蒙，你好！有何消息？

艾德蒙：沒有消息，父親。

葛勞塞斯特：你何以藏起那封信？

艾德蒙：這沒什麼，父親。

葛勞塞斯特：那你何以藏起它？讓我看看。

艾德蒙：我請求你，父親，原諒我，此乃我的兄長所書，我尚未讀完內容。從我目前讀完的內容看來，我發現這並非你意欲所見。

葛勞塞斯特：把信給我，先生！

艾德蒙：為了我的兄長好，希望他寫這封信只是為了考驗我的德行。

葛勞塞斯特（大聲讀信）：「過度尊崇老人只會使我們在黃金年華煎熬度日，使我們在老到無法享用之後才得到財富！我開始感到自己被年老的暴君壓迫，他並非憑他的能力在統治，而是因為我的容忍。快來找我，好讓我與你詳談此事。倘若我們的父親將沉睡到我喚醒他為止，你將可永世享有他一半的財富，並可擁有你兄長對你的愛，艾德加。」這會是他親筆所寫嗎？他有此等的智力嗎？這是你何時收到的？

艾德蒙：有人從我窗戶扔進來的。

葛勞塞斯特：這確為艾德加的字跡！

艾德蒙：希望他此言是有口無心。

葛勞塞斯特：他先前是否曾提及此事？

艾德蒙：從未提及，父親，但是我聽他說過在兒子長大成人而父親年邁之後，金錢應交由兒子管理。

葛勞塞斯特：喔，這個逆子！此即他在信中所言。天理難容的逆子！你去找他來，我要逮捕他。他身在何處？

艾德蒙：這我不得而知，父親，但是我願以性命擔保他的名譽。或許他並非危險人物，只是在考驗我對你的愛。

葛勞塞斯特：你是這麼認為？

艾德蒙：倘若你也認同此一構想，我願安排你側聽我們談論此事，屆時你我便可知曉真相。

葛勞塞斯特：他不可能如此禽獸不如。

艾德蒙：我確信他不會如此。

葛勞塞斯特：——如此對待他的父親，枉我全心全意地疼愛他。艾德蒙，你去找他，我必須確定他的清白！

艾德蒙：我去找他之後再向你稟報。

葛勞塞斯特：去試探他，艾德蒙——但是務必小心行事。

（葛勞塞斯特下。過了一會兒，艾德加上。）

艾德加：你好，艾德蒙弟弟！你何以表情如此不悅？

艾德蒙：你最後一次見到父親是何時？

艾德加：昨晚。

艾德蒙：你有與他談話嗎？

艾德加：有的，談了兩小時。

艾德蒙：他有露出任何不悅的神情嗎？

艾德加：完全沒有。

艾德蒙：你不知為何觸怒了他，我勸你還是暫且回避他，等到
他的怒氣平息了再說。

艾德加：想必是有惡徒冤枉了我！

艾德蒙：我恐怕是如此，但我還是建議你暫且與他保持距離，
直到他的心情平復為止。跟我去我的住處吧，我會尋覓合
適的時機讓你側聽他的說法。請你前去吧，這是我的鑰匙。
倘若你要外出，切記配戴武器。

艾德加：你是說配戴武器？

艾德蒙：兄長，這是最好的做法。請你快去吧！

艾德加：你會很快捎信給我嗎？

艾德蒙：我會儘快的，交給我處理。（艾德加下，艾德蒙自言自語。）
父親真容易上當！而我高尚的兄長亦有善良的天性，不會去
懷疑任何人。此事做來容易！我無論如何都能取得繼承權。

（艾德蒙下。）

●第三場 ———————————— P. 025

（阿爾邦尼公爵宮殿的一個房間；貢納莉與奧斯華上。）

貢納莉：我父王因我的軍官戲弄了他的弄臣而懲處他嗎？

奧斯華：是的，夫人。

貢納莉（生氣）：士可忍，孰不可忍！他的騎士行為不端，而他卻為了一點瑣事斥責我們。等他狩獵回來，我必不見他，就說我病了吧。

奧斯華：他來了，夫人，我聽見他的聲音了。

（狩獵號角聲響起。）

貢納莉：你想如何無禮都隨意。倘若他不喜歡，就讓他去我妹妹那兒吧；我們姊妹協議好不向他屈服。那個蠢老頭，他自以為給出去的東西還能歸他所管。

奧斯華：好的，夫人。

貢納莉：對他的騎士們要更顯冷淡，吩咐其他僕人們也比照辦理。我即刻修書給我妹妹，請她仿照處理。準備晚餐吧。

（他們下。）

（在阿爾邦尼宮殿的另一個房間；偽裝身分的肯特上。）

肯特：倘若我偽裝我的聲音和相貌，我的計畫即可成功。我繼續服侍我的主人，而不被驅逐出境，或許我摯愛的主人會發現我仍是他的忠僕。

（狩獵的號角聲宣告李爾的到來，他的騎士們與侍從們尾隨而上。）

李爾：說吧！你是何人？

肯特：一介平民，陛下。

李爾：你面見朕的意圖何在？

肯特：工作機會。

李爾：為誰工作？

肯特：你。

李爾：你能提供什麼服務？

肯特：我能保守秘密、騎馬、跑步、把好故事說得亂七八糟、以及直言不諱地傳遞直白的信息。我最大的優點是決心過人。

李爾：隨朕來，你就當朕的僕人吧。倘若我在用完晚膳之後滿意你，你就能永久留在朕的身邊。（對一名侍從：）把我的傻子找來。（一名侍從下，奧斯華上。）你這傢伙，朕的女兒何在？

奧斯華（與他擦肩而過）：小的告退。（他下。）

李爾：他說了什麼？叫那個呆瓜回來！（一名騎士追上前去。）我的傻子在哪兒？似乎全世界都睡著了。（騎士再上。）說吧！那個雜種何在？

騎士：陛下，他說令嬡病了。

李爾：他為何未能應朕的召喚而回來？

騎士：陛下，他無禮地說他不回來。

李爾：他不回來？

騎士：陛下，我不清楚究竟怎麼回事——但是在我看來，陛下已不如從前那般受到尊重了。當陛下遭受不當的待遇時，我忠於職守不得不直言。

李爾：你只是說出朕內心的想法罷了，此事我會再行調查。（對侍從：）去告訴朕的女兒說朕要見她，也把朕的傻子找來。（侍從下，奧斯華再上。）你過來，這位先生。你可知朕是何人？

奧斯華：我家夫人的父親。

李爾：「我家夫人的父親！」你這骯髒的狗！畜牲！

奧斯華：這是不實的指稱，陛下。

李爾：你膽敢反駁朕，你這惡徒？

（他生氣地打了奧斯華。）

奧斯華：你不能打我，陛下。

肯特（絆倒他）：難道也不能絆倒你嗎？

（奧斯華跌倒在地。）

李爾（對肯特）：感謝你，朋友，你是朕的僕人，朕會妥善照顧你。

肯特（對奧斯華）：來吧，先生，起來！我來教訓你如何恪守本分！走！

（他將奧斯華推出去。）

李爾：朕忠實的新僕人，感謝你，這是你盡忠職守的獎賞。

（李爾賞錢給肯特。傻子上。）

李爾：嗨，可愛的朋友，你好嗎？

傻子（對肯特）：先生，你來幫我拿著帽子吧。

（傻子將他的弄臣帽交予肯特。）

肯特：怎麼，傻子？

傻子：哎呀，支持失了寵的人！倘若你不支持贏家，你未幾即
　　將遭到冷落。

李爾：謹言慎行，先生，否則你將會受到責罰！

傻子：實話是被送進狗舍中的狗，會遭到鞭打；但阿諛奉承是
　　雜種狗，能站在火堆旁發臭。

李爾（想起他如何因考狄利婭說了實話而將她驅逐出境）：此乃給
　　朕的一杯苦酒！

傻子：你知道悲苦的傻子和甜蜜的傻子有何區別嗎？

李爾：不知道，小伙子，告訴朕吧。

傻子：勸諫你交出國土的臣子，讓他過來我身邊，你就取代他
　　的位置吧，如此甜蜜和悲苦的傻子未幾即可出現。一個是
　　這位穿著傻子衣服的人──另一個是站在那兒的人！（他指
　　著李爾表示他是悲苦的傻子。）

李爾：你說朕是傻子嗎，孩子？

傻子：你已拋棄了自己所有其他的頭銜——此乃你與生俱來的頭銜。

肯特：他並不全然是傻子，閣下。

傻子：是啊，說得對。老伯，給我一枚雞蛋，我就給你兩個王冠。

李爾：何以是兩個王冠？

傻子：哎呀，待我將雞蛋切成兩半、吃掉了蛋黃，就有一分為二的蛋殼了！還記得你將王冠切成兩半分別交予他人嗎？當你將黃金的王冠交出去時，你脫去王冠的禿腦袋是不理智的。若說我現在說話像個傻子，就讓他挨鞭子。

李爾：倘若你在撒謊，先生，你就要被鞭打了。

傻子：我甚為訝異你和你的兩個女兒竟是如此相似；她們會因我說實話而鞭打我，而你會因我撒謊而鞭打我！我寧可只當個傻子就好了，但是我不會想成為你，老伯，你已將你的腦袋一分為二，中間已是空蕩一片。你瞧！其中一半來了。

（貢納莉上。）

李爾：女兒，何以愁眉苦臉？

貢納莉：你那些無禮的隨從們無時無刻不在鬥嘴爭吵，甚至起而暴動。我認為我第一次稟告父王時，你就應該處理此事了，然而如今看來你不僅默許，甚至還鼓勵此般行為。

李爾：你真是朕的女兒嗎？

貢納莉：好了，父親！我知道你理智尚存，希望你能善加利用，停止近日的這般荒誕言行。

李爾：在場有人認識朕嗎？李爾是這樣走路的嗎？是這樣說話的嗎？誰能告訴朕，朕到底是誰？朕倒是很想知道！據朕所知和據理而論，朕怕自己誤以為朕有女兒了。

貢納莉：父親，此景此情與你平常的惡作劇無異。請你諒解我，因你年邁而德高望重，請你要睿智。你在此處留有百名騎士與隨從，這些人無法無天、醉酒鬧事又行徑粗魯，致使我們的宮廷──受到他們的言行影響──好似喧鬧的客棧，成了酒館，而非莊重的宮殿。此風不可長！請你將侍從的數量減半，僅留與你年齡相仿者──能夠自制和控制住你的人。

李爾：黑暗的惡魔啊！為朕的馬套上鞍！集結朕的人馬！你這忘恩負義的逆女！朕不在此叨擾你了，朕還有另一個女兒！（阿爾邦尼上。）喔，先生，你來了！這可是你做的好事？說吧，先生。（對他的僕人們：）為朕備馬。

阿爾邦尼：請你冷靜點，陛下。

李爾（對貢納莉）：兀鷹！你滿口謊言！朕部隊中皆為高尚之人，他們自知職責何在，舉止亦是不失體面。喔，考狄莉亞的一個小缺失，何以看似如此醜陋！抽乾了我內心的愛，使我變得冷酷。

（肯特與騎士們下。）

阿爾邦尼：陛下，請恕我無罪，因我不知你是如何受到冒犯。

李爾：就當是如此吧，閣下。（轉向貢納莉：）有個忘恩負義的逆女，比毒蛇的尖牙更銳利啊！

（李爾下，情緒激動。）

阿爾邦尼：此事是何來由？

貢納莉：你不必費心去查明了，就讓年邁的他情緒反覆無常吧。

（李爾再上。）

李爾：怎麼，瞬間裁撤了朕的五十名隨從？才短短兩星期？

阿爾邦尼：怎麼回事，陛下？

李爾：朕會告訴你的。（對貢納莉：）生死交關！朕恥於你如此打擊朕的自尊，彷彿你值得朕流淌這些炙熱淚水。讓暴風雨和濃霧籠罩你吧，但願一位父親的詛咒，能刺穿你所有感官，留下深刻的傷口。這昏花的老眼啊，倘若你們再這麼哭下去，朕就將你們挖出來扔在地上踩爛！果真事已至此嗎？那就這樣吧，朕還有另一個女兒！相信她會善良地撫慰吾心。

（李爾、肯特與侍從們下。）

貢納莉：你看見了嗎？

阿爾邦尼：儘管我是如此地愛你，貢納莉，我仍無法相信……

貢納莉（打斷他的話）：夠了。（大聲喊：）奧斯華！過來！（對傻子：）隨你的主人而去吧。

傻子：李爾老伯，帶著傻子一起去吧！

（傻子追著李爾跑走。）

貢納莉（諷刺地）：我已經勸告了我父親。一百名騎士！是啊！在所有的抱怨或不悅之後，他能動用他們的力量支持他的老糊塗，任意擺布我們的性命。

阿爾邦尼：可能是你顧慮太多了。

貢納莉：這總好過太過於信任吧。我深知他的心意，並已寫信給我的妹妹，將他方才所說的話告知予她。倘若她不聽我的勸說，收容了他和他的一百名騎士……（奧斯華再上。）好了，奧斯華！你是否拿到了那封要交予我妹妹的信？

奧斯華：是的，夫人。

貢納莉：帶著幾個人和你一起騎馬去吧，將我的擔憂悉數告訴她，再加上你自己的理由去說服她。去吧，速去速回！（奧斯華下。）如你此般的溫吞個性，我的夫君，雖然我並未責怪你──但是我真的不以為然。

阿爾邦尼：你此言是否成理，我不得而知。有些事還是少管為妙。

貢納莉：那好吧。

阿爾邦尼：好了，我們就靜觀其變吧。

（他們下。）

●第五場 ────────────────────── P. 038

（在阿爾邦尼公爵宮殿的一個房間；李爾、肯特與傻子上。）

李爾：帶著這封信去找葛勞塞斯特。

肯特：我在將信送達之前決不闔眼。

（肯特下。）

傻子：你會發現你的另一個女兒也會如是待你。我所知之事必定知無不言。

李爾：你能告訴朕什麼，孩子？

傻子：我能告訴你為何蝸牛有個房子。

李爾：為什麼？

傻子：為了裝進牠的腦袋——而不是將房子交給牠的兩個女兒，讓自己無家可歸。

李爾：如此寬容的父親啊！朕的馬匹備好了嗎？

傻子：你的手下正在準備。

李爾：朕誓將奪回朕的王國！

傻子：倘若你是我的傻子，老伯，我會因你提早老邁而毆打你一頓。

李爾：此話怎講？

傻子：你不應該在你變得睿智之前就先變得老邁。

李爾：喔，切莫讓朕發狂，親愛的老天爺！讓朕保持頭腦清楚，朕不想發瘋啊！（一名紳士上。）馬匹備好了嗎？

紳士：備好了，陛下。

李爾（對傻子）：走吧，孩子。

（他們下。）

第二幕

●第一場 ———————————————————— P. 041

（葛勞塞斯特伯爵的城堡；艾德蒙與庫朗上。）

庫朗：我已告知你的父親，康沃爾公爵和里根今晚將會來訪。

艾德蒙：此乃所為何事？

庫朗：我不知道，你有聽到傳聞嗎？

艾德蒙：沒有，什麼傳聞？

庫朗：你沒聽說康沃爾與阿爾邦尼兩位公爵可能會開戰？

艾德蒙：未曾聽聞。

庫朗：你即將聽聞，此乃無庸置疑。再會了，先生。

（庫朗下。）

艾德蒙：公爵今晚將來訪？甚好！正合我的計畫。我父親已藏匿好準備側聽我兄長說話。（看到艾德加上，從樓梯走過來。）有件事我要先行完成。兄長，借一步說話！（對觀眾：）我父親正在看著！（對艾德加低語：）兄長，逃跑吧！你的藏身之處已被發現。你近來可有說起康沃爾的壞話？他今晚要來訪，和里根一起。你是否說了什麼鼓勵他與阿爾邦尼爭論的話？

艾德加：沒有，隻字未提。

艾德蒙：我聽見父親的腳步聲了。原諒我，我必須假裝拔劍揮向你。（他拔劍。）你也拔劍，佯裝要打鬥。（艾德加在困惑之餘照他的話去做。）全力以赴！（說得很大聲好讓葛勞塞斯特聽見。）投降吧！（他們繼續假裝打鬥。艾德蒙對艾德加低語。）快跑吧，兄長。再會了！（艾德加跑走。）我身上有血跡才表示我方才奮力抵抗。（他割傷自己的手臂。）父親！父親！（追著艾德加大喊：）站住！站住！沒人幫幫我嗎？

（葛勞塞斯特上，帶著手持火炬的僕人們。）

葛勞塞斯特：好了，艾德蒙，那個惡徒何在？

艾德蒙：你看，父親，我在流血！

葛勞塞斯特：那個惡徒何在，艾德蒙？

艾德蒙（指）：他往那個方向逃走了，父親。

葛勞塞斯特：追上去，快！走！

（僕人們下，追捕艾德加。）

艾德蒙：他試圖要我殺害你，但是我告訴他復仇心重的眾神會嚴懲弒親之人。當他看到我堅決反對他的計畫時，他就拔劍割傷了我的手臂，於是我防禦自己，讓他逃跑了。

葛勞塞斯特：無論他逃到天涯海角，但凡在這片土地上他必不得自由，我一定要找到他，並且殺了他！

艾德蒙：當我說我要揭露他的陰謀時，他說：「誰會相信你？我會否認所有的指控，悉數栽贓予你——即便你拿出我的親筆信！任何白癡都看得出來，我死了你便能得利。」

葛勞塞斯特：他不再是我的兒子！我要廣發那個惡徒的畫像，讓全國人民都看到。我也會安排你繼承我的土地，我忠誠的兒子。（號角聲響起。）聽！公爵的號角聲。

（康沃爾、里根與侍從們上。）

康沃爾：你好，我高貴的朋友！我剛聽聞了怪消息。

里根：倘若真有此事，再冷血的復仇也不嫌多。閣下可安好？

葛勞塞斯特：夫人，我這年邁的心已然破碎！

里根：是我父親的義子意欲取你性命嗎？是你的艾德加嗎？

葛勞塞斯特：羞愧地恨不得掩蓋這個事實！

里根：他是否和效忠於我父親的暴戾騎士們在一起？

葛勞塞斯特：我不知道，夫人。

艾德蒙：是的，夫人，他是和他們在一起。

里根：那就難怪他會如此忤逆了。他們要求他計畫謀害老父親的性命，好讓他揮霍老父親的財富。今日黃昏時分我姊姊才向我提及他們——她警告我若是他們要求在我這兒留宿，我必不能應允。

康沃爾：我也不同意，里根，我向你保證。艾德蒙，聽聞你是孝順父親的好兒子。

艾德蒙：此乃我的本分所在，閣下。

葛勞塞斯特：他揭露了艾德加的陰謀，因意圖逮捕他而被他所傷。

康沃爾：有人去追捕艾德加嗎？

葛勞塞斯特：有的，我的好閣下。

康沃爾：他若是被逮捕，就莫要再懼怕他，我的資源隨你使用。至於你，艾德蒙，你從今爾後就為我效力吧，我最需要如你這般忠實又可靠的人才。

艾德蒙（鞠躬）：我聽候你的差遣，閣下。

康沃爾：我們今日來訪是有要事。

里根：我們的父親寫了信——我的姊姊也寫了信——提到了一些爭執，我意欲離家之後再回覆他；信差們在等待我的回信。我們的好友，此事我們亟需你的忠告。

葛勞塞斯特：我願效犬馬之勞，夫人。

（號角聲響起，全體下。）

●第二場 ——————————————— P. 047

（在葛勞塞斯特的城堡前面；肯特與奧斯華相遇。）

肯特：我認識你。你是個惡棍、無賴和懦夫！

奧斯華：哎呀，你這個人實在太惡劣，竟然對你全然陌生之人口出此言！

肯特：你這惡徒莫要否認你與我相識！我不是兩天前才在國王面前打了你，還絆倒了你嗎？拔劍吧，你這流氓！（他拔劍。）拔劍！

奧斯華：你走！我與你毫無瓜葛！

肯特：拔劍，你這無賴！你帶著對國王不利的信件來此，還幫著你家夫人對付她的父王。拔劍，你這流氓！

奧斯華：救命！殺人了！救命！

肯特：打鬥啊，你這懦夫！打鬥啊！

（肯特用他的劍面擊打奧斯華。）

奧斯華：救命！殺人了！殺人了！

（艾德蒙、康沃爾、里根、葛勞塞斯特與僕人們上。）

葛勞塞斯特：武器！打鬥！這是怎麼回事？

里根：他們是我姊姊和國王派來的信差。

康沃爾：你們為何事爭執？快說。

肯特：沒有人如我與這惡徒一般彼此仇視。

康沃爾（對奧斯華）：你對他做了什麼？

奧斯華：沒有，是日前的一場誤會致使他絆倒我。當我跌倒在地時，他羞辱我，然後他在國王面前逞英雄，讓國王誇讚他制伏了一個無意與他打鬥之人。他在前次的詭計成功之後，又在此地拔劍揮向我。

康沃爾：將刑具抬上來！你這固執的惡徒，我要給你一點教訓！

肯特：閣下，我年紀已長，學不到教訓，切莫將你的刑具用在我身上。我效力於國王，你對他的信差用刑，就是對國王的不敬。

康沃爾：去取刑具！真是的，就讓他在此處坐到正午吧。

里根：坐到正午？到晚上吧，我的夫君！

肯特：哎呀，夫人，即便我是你父親的狗，你也不應如此待我。

里根：先生，既然你是他的奴僕，我就會如此待你。

（僕人們帶著刑具上。）

葛勞塞斯特：請求閣下莫要這樣做。他縱有疏失，國王自會懲處他，刑具是用在竊賊和其他卑鄙的傢伙身上。

康沃爾：有事由我負責。

里根：我姊姊可能不會想聽到，她的僕人奧斯華因替她辦事而被人污蔑。把他的雙腿套進去。

（肯特被套上刑具。）

康沃爾：走吧，閣下。

（全體下，獨留葛勞塞斯特與肯特。）

葛勞塞斯特：我很同情你，朋友。此乃公爵的一時衝動，眾所周知他有多固執。我會為你求情的。

肯特：萬萬不可，先生。我會花點時間睡覺，剩餘的時間就吹吹口哨；即使是個好人也偶爾會遭逢厄運。祝你日安！

葛勞塞斯特：此事乃公爵之不是，必不能善罷甘休。

（葛勞塞斯特下。）

肯特：我知道考狄利婭知曉我偽裝身分之事，她會在這惡劣的情勢中找到最好的時機平反冤屈。沉重的眼睛，莫要凝視這可恥的刑具。晚安了，命運！再笑一個，然後再轉動你的滾輪吧！

（他睡著。）

●第三場 ————————————— P. 051

（開闊的鄉間；艾德加上，自言自語。）

艾德加：聽聞我被人稱作亡命之徒，為躲避追捕而藏身於這中空的樹幹裡。所有的海港皆防衛森嚴，無不緊密防守只為逮捕我。趁著我還能逃跑之際，我要偽裝自己，在臉上塗滿污泥、穿上襤褸衣衫、揉成滿頭亂髮。這國家四處可見發狂的乞丐在吼叫，將大頭針、串肉籤和鐵釘刺進他們裸露的手臂，然後用瘋言瘋語的咒罵和禱告的話語，在簡陋的農場和貧窮的村莊乞討。（他佯裝成發瘋的乞丐在說話。）窮酸湯姆！（用他正常的聲音。）我只能如此了。身為艾德加，我一無所有。

（艾德加下。）

（在葛勞塞斯特的城堡前面；肯特被上了刑具；李爾與傻子上。）

李爾：太奇怪了，他們竟未遣返朕的信差便這樣出門了。

紳士：我聽聞他們是倉促離開的。

肯特：你好，國王陛下！

李爾：怎麼，你以如此受辱為嗜好嗎？

肯特：不是的，陛下。

李爾：是誰如此待你？

肯特：有兩個人──你的半子和女兒。

李爾：他們不會這麼做，他們不可能！如此苛待國王的人，簡直比殺人更惡劣。

肯特：陛下，當我將你的信交予他們時，有另一名信差亦抵達他們府上。他跑得氣喘吁吁，捎來他的女主人貢納莉的信息。他送來的信件，他們立即拆閱，讀罷就召喚他們的僕人們即刻備馬出行。他們要我隨之而去，待他們有空時再寫信回覆，還對我冷漠以待。我在此地遇見另外那位信差，我發現是因為他受到熱情接待才害得我遭人冷落；他就是日前對陛下失禮的那個人。我在一時不平之下喪失了理智，於是拔劍相向，他懦弱地大聲呼救，你的半子和女兒認定我因此事而理應受到如是的羞辱對待。

李爾：喔，朕的內心悲傷難抑啊！朕的這個女兒何在？

肯特：和公爵在一起，陛下，正在屋內。

李爾：朕去找她談談。

（李爾下。）

傻子：你可以從螞蟻身上學到教訓——為明知必將失敗的事而努力，是不會有所獲的；切莫緊抓著滾下坡的巨大滾輪——你可能會為了追上它而折斷頸項。等他日有智者給你更好的忠告，再退回我的吧。

（李爾再上，帶著葛勞塞斯特。）

李爾：拒絕和朕談話！他們自稱疲累和身體不適？他們徹夜奔波勞累？全都是藉口——此乃叛逆和遺棄之表徵。再給我一個更好的答覆。

葛勞塞斯特：我親愛的陛下，你也知道公爵有多固執。

李爾：固執？哎呀，葛勞塞斯特，朕是有事想找康沃爾公爵夫婦相談啊。

葛勞塞斯特：我的好陛下，我已告知他們了。

李爾：「告知」他們！你有聽懂朕的話嗎？

葛勞塞斯特：有的，我的好陛下。

李爾：國王意欲與康沃爾相談；親愛的父親想找他的女兒聊聊，朕命令她服從。此話你有告知他倆嗎？豈有此理！（看著刑具加身的肯特又更生氣。）朕的王權已死！他為何坐在此處？卸除朕的僕人身上的刑具！去告訴公爵和他的夫人，朕命令他們馬上前來相談！

（葛勞塞斯特下。）

李爾：哎呀！朕心中的怒火難平！但是要冷靜！

傻子：命令它平靜吧，老伯，如同廚子將鰻魚活活下鍋時那般，拿木棍擊打之後大喊：「平靜吧，你們這些動物們，平靜！」

（康沃爾、里根、葛勞塞斯特與僕人們上；肯特獲釋。）

里根：我很高興能見到陛下。

李爾：里根，朕知道你很高興。（對肯特：）喔，你獲釋了？朕改天再與你談論此事。（肯特下。）親愛的里根，你姊姊居心不良，她刻薄的話語有如兀鷹一般啃噬著朕的心。喔，里根！

里根：我懇求你耐心等待，父王。我無法相信我的姊姊會不服從你；倘若她約束你隨從們的暴動舉止，那你就應該誇讚她，而非責罵她。

李爾：朕詛咒她！

里根：喔，父王，你年事已高，已至遲暮之年，應該要由比你更瞭解你自己的智者來引導你，因此我請求你回到姊姊府上，向你冤枉她之事向她道歉。

李爾：請求她的原諒？看看朕如何表示忠誠！（他下跪。）「親愛的女兒，朕承認吾已年邁，歲月不饒人。朕跪地懇求你賞賜衣食和床榻。」

里根：好父王，莫要再出此言！此乃卑鄙的伎倆，回去我姊姊的府上吧。

李爾（起身）：辦不到，里根！她裁撤了朕一半的侍從、對朕冷漠以待、甚至口出無禮之言。但願眾神懲罰她終身殘廢！

里根：喔，眾神！當你心情不佳之時，你也要詛咒我嗎？

李爾：不，里根，朕絕不會詛咒你，你溫和的天性是不可能變壞的。她的眼神充滿暴戾，但是你的眼神如此溫暖。你生來就不會剝奪朕的快樂，你懂得知恩圖報，未曾忘記朕贈與你的半壁江山。

里根：好父王，有話請直說。

李爾：是誰給朕的僕人套上刑具？

（號角聲響起。）

康沃爾：那是何人的號角聲？

里根：是我姊姊的，她在信上提過她未幾即將來訪。（奧斯華上。）你家夫人到了嗎？

李爾（對著奧斯華蹙眉）：就是這個卑鄙之人害得朕的僕人被套上刑具！里根，朕相信你對此事並非一無所知。（貢納莉走上前來。）那是何人？喔，天啊！倘若你心疼老人家，請幫幫朕！（對貢納莉：）你不覺得自己可恥嗎？（兩姐妹相互擁抱。）喔，里根，你會握她的手嗎？

貢納莉：何以不能握我的手，父王？我做了什麼事冒犯你嗎？

李爾（以手捧心）：此事難道沒完沒了？（對康沃爾：）何以朕的僕人被施以刑具？

康沃爾：是我命他坐在此處，陛下，以他的行徑此乃罪有應得。

李爾：你！是你嗎？

里根：父王，你已年邁體虛就要認份，回到我姊姊府上住完這個月吧——裁撤你半數的守衛——然後再來我這兒。

李爾：回到她那兒，並裁撤五十個人？不，朕寧可拒絕所有的收容，餐風露宿，與野狼和貓頭鷹為伍。回到她那兒？哎呀，朕不如到法王面前下跪，像個可憐的鄉紳似地乞求他給朕活下去的養老金！回到她那兒？這倒像是要朕去給這個可憎的僕人當奴隸。（他指著奧斯華。）

貢納莉：這是你的選擇，父王。

李爾：朕懇求你，女兒，切莫激怒朕。朕不會麻煩你，孩子。再見了，你我永世不再相會，永生不再見面，但你仍是朕的親骨肉，或者應該說是朕骨血中的疾病，像個疗子、瘟疫的腫瘡，是朕血液中的腫瘤！但是朕不會責罵你，你早晚會自蒙其辱。朕可以耐心等候，可以住在里根這兒——朕和朕的一百名騎士。

里根：那倒不盡然，尚未到你在此居住的時刻，我並未準備好合適的接待儀式。聽我姊姊的話，她言之有理。

李爾：你確定嗎？

里根：非常確定，父王。怎麼，五十名隨從？難道還不夠嗎？你何以需要更多？一個房子怎麼住得了如此多人，還能同時聽兩人發號施令又和睦相處？

貢納莉：你就不能讓她的僕人或我的僕人服侍你嗎，父王？

里根：有何不可，父王？倘若他們對你有所怠慢，我們可以即刻糾正他們。倘若你住到我的府上，我會要求你只帶二十五人前來，再多就恕我不招待了。

李爾：什麼？朕將一切都給了你——

里根：你在這方面倒是好整以暇！

李爾：——但條件是，我要有一百名騎士當侍從。怎麼？要朕帶二十五人前來與你同住？里根，你是這麼説的嗎？

里根：我可以再說一次，多帶的人恕我不招待。

李爾：相較於更邪惡之人，有些邪惡之徒是披上羊皮的狼。（對
　　　貢納莉：）朕隨你去，你的五十人是她二十五人的兩倍，所以
　　　你的愛亦為她的兩倍。

貢納莉：聽我說，父王，在我們府上有兩倍的人聽你差遣，你
　　　何以需要二十五人、十人，抑或是五人來服侍你？

里根：需要侍從的原因究竟為何呢？

李爾：別提什麼需要與否，即使最窮困的乞丐也有身外長物。
　　　倘若你不滿足朕的需求，朕的人生就與野獸無異。倘若你
　　　衣著只為保暖，你就不需要那些根本不能保暖的華服美裳
　　　了。天啊！請賜與朕多點耐心吧！你們也看到朕了，眾神啊，
　　　朕是個可憐的老頭，非但年邁體衰，內心也愁苦萬分！喔，

傻子，朕要發瘋了！

（李爾下，葛勞塞斯特、紳士與傻子尾隨而下；遠方傳來暴風雨聲。）

康沃爾：我們進屋去吧，暴風雨將至。

里根：我們這個小廟容不下老頭那尊大佛和他的隨從們。

貢納莉：那是他咎由自取。他自己生悶氣，所以他必須為自己愚蠢的行徑付出代價。

里根：就他一個人，我會欣然接待他，但即使多一個隨從也不可。

貢納莉：我亦有同感。

（葛勞塞斯特再上。）

葛勞塞斯特：國王目前是暴怒難抑。

貢納莉：閣下，切莫請求他留在此處。

葛勞塞斯特：但是時已入夜，而且暴風雨將至。

里根：倔強之人就要從自己的錯誤中學習。關閉你的門戶，他的隨從們皆是亡命之徒，天曉得他們會唆使他做出什麼事？

貢納莉：關閉你的門戶，今晚天候惡劣。里根言之有理，去躲避暴風雨吧。

（全體下。）

第三幕

● 第一場 ———————————————————— P. 063

（暴風雨中的一處荒野，雷電交加；肯特與一名紳士上。）

肯特：國王何在？

紳士：在和惡劣的天氣吵架。他要求風將陸地吹向海洋，或是使海浪拍岸淹沒大地；他扯斷頭上的白髮，只因風吹髮絲飄揚；他試圖在風雨中昂首闊步；而今晚——即使是熊、獅子和野狼皆在躲避暴風雨之際——他仍未戴帽在外奔跑，拼命地大喊大叫。

肯特：但是何人陪在他身邊？

紳士：只有傻子。

肯特：閣下，我告訴你一件重要的事，雖然他們秘而不宣，但是在阿爾邦尼和康沃爾之間存在著歧見。他們有看似忠誠的僕人們，但是那些僕人其實是法王派來的探子。這些僕人們探知兩位公爵的爭執，以及他們對待善良老國王的可鄙方式，再向法王回報。事實上，法王已派出軍隊前來此分裂的王國，他們已然秘密抵達我們的幾個良港。倘若你趕往多佛，那兒的人必會感謝你忠實稟告國王受到不合常理又使人發瘋的痛苦。我是個擁有貴族血統的紳士，告知你此事乃基於可靠的消息來源。為了證明我不似外表看來這般身分低微，請打開這個錢包取走其內之物。當你見到考狄利婭時，讓她看看這枚戒指，她會將我的身分告知予你。這該死的暴風雨！我們去找國王吧，你往那邊，我往這邊；不論是何人先見到他，就大聲告知另一人。

（兩人下。）

167

（在荒野中的另一處，暴風雨繼續肆虐；李爾與傻子上。）

李爾：吹啊，狂風，吹裂你的雙頰！怒吼！吹啊！陣陣迸發的閃電，燒焦朕花白的頭髮吧！

傻子：喔，老伯，在屋裡避雨聽人巧言奉承，好過在外頭淋這場雨啊！進屋去──請求你的兩個女兒原諒你吧，這一夜對智者或傻子皆毫無憐憫之情。

李爾：大火肆虐！大雨傾盆！雨、風、雷、火──他們皆非朕的女兒！朕並未指責你這惡劣的天氣，亦未將王國賜與你或稱你為子女，你未有任何事虧欠朕，因此你盡可為所欲為！

（偽裝的肯特上。）

肯特：哎呀，陛下，你竟然在此？既便是喜好在夜晚行動的動物，也不會喜歡此般惡劣的夜晚。這風雨交加的夜空，能令最狂野的動物驚恐萬分，使牠們不得不藏匿於洞穴中。我未曾見過如此狂烈的暴風雨！

李爾：就讓偉大的眾神，我們頭頂上這恐怖噪音的製造者，指認出他們的敵人吧。（他脫帽證明他無所畏懼。）朕是受人陷害，而非犯罪之人。

肯特：哎呀，你竟脫了帽子！我仁慈的陛下，附近有一座棚子可借你暫避暴風雨。我這就返回你那硬心腸的府上，強硬要求它那鐵石心腸的主人們知情識禮。

李爾：那座棚子何在，我的朋友？需求乃怪異之事，能使卑微之物顯得珍貴。帶路吧，領我去棚子躲避風雨。

（他們下。）

（在葛勞塞斯特城堡的一個房間；葛勞塞斯特與艾德蒙上，手持火炬。）

葛勞塞斯特：此般行徑實在不合常理！他們命令我不許再提及他、代他求情，抑或是以任何方式幫助他。

艾德蒙：最是野蠻和不合常理之舉！

葛勞塞斯特：噓！莫再多言。兩位公爵起了爭執，還有更糟的事：我今夜收到一封信，透露其內容就會有危險；我已將信件鎖在我的臥房內。國王所蒙受的冤屈終將悉數報復，已有部分軍隊抵達此地，我們必須支持國王，我會找到他，並且秘密地協助他。你繼續和公爵談話，艾德蒙，免得他發現我不見蹤跡。倘若他問起我，就說我臥病在床。即使要我丟了性命，我也必須幫助國王。怪異之事必然會發生，請你務必小心，艾德蒙。

（葛勞塞斯特前去尋找李爾。）

艾德蒙：我要將此事告知予公爵──還有那封信的事，我會得到我父親所失去的──悉數奪回！過時者會被淘汰，新興者將取而代之。

（艾德蒙下。）

●第四場

（在棚子前面的荒野中，暴風雨繼續肆虐；李爾、仍偽裝的肯特與傻子上。）

肯特：就是此處，陛下，請進。

李爾：你很介意這場暴風雨讓我們全身濕透，這對你而言很重要，然而在更大的苦難面前，較輕微的苦難就幾乎感覺不到了。朕內心的暴風雨使朕喪失了所有感覺，只剩下折磨朕的痛苦──朕的兩個女兒忘恩負義！彷彿朕的嘴因朕的手取食物送進口中而咬它。朕必徹底懲罰！但是朕將不再哭泣。如此在黑夜中將朕困於屋外！（對暴風雨：）傾瀉而下吧──朕承受得住！喔，里根！貢納莉！你們慈悲的老父親，他心胸寬大地給了你們一切啊！

肯特：我的好陛下，請進來吧。

李爾（對傻子）：進去吧，孩子，你先請，我來禱告，然後再就寢。

（傻子進棚子裡。）

艾德加（從棚子內假裝發瘋似地說話）：窮酸湯姆！窮酸湯姆！

（傻子奪門而出。）

傻子：切莫進去，老伯，那裡面有鬼！他說他叫窮酸湯姆。

肯特：在棚子內的是何人？出來。

（艾德加現身，偽裝成一個瘋子。）

艾德加：走開！有邪魔在跟著我！

李爾：你也將一切給了你的女兒們嗎？

艾德加：誰會給窮酸湯姆任何東西？邪魔領著他走過火堆和沼澤，他將刀子置於枕頭下，將毒藥放在他的湯旁邊。（**他攻擊幻想的敵人。**）我現在就能抓住他——還有那裡——那裡又有了！

（**暴風雨繼續肆虐。**）

李爾：他亦是被他的女兒們逼瘋的嗎？你一無所有嗎？也悉數賜予她們？

傻子：他搶回了一條毛毯，那是他身上僅有的衣物。

李爾：但願空氣中的瘟疫全落在你的女兒們身上！

肯特：他沒有女兒，陛下。

李爾：除非是被他的不孝女兒所害，否則他不可能落得如此悲慘之下場！被遺棄的父親要忍受此般骨肉背離的傷痛，難道現下已蔚為風氣？真是公平的懲罰啊！那些弒父的女兒可都是我們親生的！

傻子：這寒夜將使我們全都變成傻子和瘋子。（**他看到葛勞塞斯特走過來，手持火炬。**）你瞧，有火光往此處移動！

李爾（**凝視著黑暗中**）：來者何人？

葛勞塞斯特：陛下，我是來幫你的，請隨我來。我因責任心的驅使而不願服從令嬡們嚴苛的命令，她們指使我鎖上門窗，讓你在這無情的夜裡自生自滅，但是我決意來此帶你去可取暖和飽餐之處。

肯特：再問他一次，閣下，他的心智已逐漸喪失。

葛勞塞斯特：這能怪得了他嗎？他的兩個女兒要他死啊。啊，那個好肯特！他早說過事情會演變至此。那個被放逐的可憐人！你說國王逐漸發瘋了，我來告訴你，朋友，我自己也幾乎要發狂。我有個已和我斷絕關係的兒子，他意欲取我性命，這是日前才發生之事！我曾經疼愛他，朋友——父親對兒子的疼愛莫過於此。事實上，我因這傷痛而幾乎要瘋狂。（暴風雨繼續肆虐。）好一個夜晚啊！（對李爾：）我請求國王陛下——

艾德加：湯姆好冷啊。

葛勞塞斯特：進棚子裡吧，朋友！進去取暖。

李爾：走吧，我們一起進去。

（他們都進棚子裡。）

●第五場 ——————————————— P. 074

（在葛勞塞斯特城堡的一個房間；康沃爾與艾德蒙上，康沃爾手裡揮
  舞著一封信。）

康沃爾：原來不只是你兄長的邪惡本性，才使得他想取你父親
  的性命；他是因你父親的叛國謀逆才被激怒。

艾德蒙：此乃家父所提及之信件，可證明他效力於法王。喔，
  天啊！倘若未曾發生此謀逆事件就好了——抑或不是被我
  所發現！若此信之內容屬實，你就有重要的事待辦了。

康沃爾（已讀完信件內容）：無論是否屬實，你已然繼承葛勞塞
  斯特伯爵之頭銜。去找你父親吧，我們要逮捕他。

艾德蒙（竊語）：倘若我發現家父在協助國王，公爵就會更加疑
  心了。（大聲說。）我會繼續效忠，縱使我身為人子應當順服
  於父親。

康沃爾：我會信任你，也承諾會比你父親更加疼愛你。

（他們下。）

●第六場 ——————————————— P. 075

（在城堡附近某農舍的一個房間；葛勞塞斯特與偽裝的肯特上。）

葛勞塞斯特：留宿於此好過餐風露宿，讓我們將此處再整理得
  更舒適一些，我不會離開太久。

肯特：他蒙受太大的壓力已經喪失神智，但願眾神回報你的
  仁慈！

（葛勞塞斯特下；艾德加、傻子與李爾上。）

李爾：朕會懲罰那兩個忘恩負義的女兒！（對艾德加：）來吧，坐這兒，你是審判官。（對傻子：）你是智者，坐這兒吧，你是另一位審判官。（對肯特：）至於你──你也坐下。（摩拳擦掌。）現在，你們這兩隻母狐狸！

艾德加（指向李爾）：瞧他如何瞠目怒視！

肯特：你可安好，陛下？切莫驚慌，你先躺下來靠著這些坐墊休息吧。

李爾：朕想先看看他們的審判過程，把證人帶過來吧。

艾德加：且讓我們公正地審判。

李爾（指向一個空座位）：先起訴她。那是貢納莉，朕當著這高尚的審判庭起誓，她欺負國王，她可憐的父親。

傻子：過來，你可是名叫貢納莉？

李爾：她無可辯駁。

傻子：抱歉，我將你誤認為是一張椅凳！

李爾：這兒還有另一個，從她醜陋的面容可看出她的心腸如何歹毒。（他激動地跳起來。）攔住她！（對艾德加：）假審判官！你讓她逃跑了！

肯特：喔，真是遺憾！陛下，你素來自命的自制力何在？

艾德加（以他真實的身分竊語）：我為他流下同情的眼淚，會毀了我的偽裝。

李爾：那幾隻小狗──瞧，牠們朝著朕吠叫。就讓牠們解剖里根，看看她的心是因何而潰爛。她們如此鐵石心腸可有任何原因？

肯特：好了，陛下，躺在這兒歇息片刻吧。

李爾（彷彿躺在家中的床上）：莫要出聲，將窗簾拉上，朕待天明之時再用晚膳。

（葛勞塞斯特再上。）

葛勞塞斯特（對肯特）：國王何在？

肯特：切莫驚動他，閣下，他已心神盡失。

葛勞塞斯特：好友，我懇求你，讓他躺在你的懷中。我無意間側聽到有人密謀要殺他；我已備好擔架，讓他躺臥於其上，送他去多佛吧，那兒有人會歡迎和保護你們。

肯特：壓力已使他精疲力竭，他現已熟睡。（對傻子：）來吧，幫我抬他上擔架。

葛勞塞斯特：來，快走！

（肯特、葛勞塞斯特與傻子將李爾抬出去。）

艾德加：當看到比我們更位高權重之人蒙受苦難時，我們自身的不幸也相形見絀了。他是飽受子女所害，一如我是飽受父親所害！湯姆，走吧！待你洗清令你蒙羞的不實指控之後，卸除你的偽裝吧。今晚無論再發生什麼事，但願國王能平安逃離！在那之前，我要繼續躲藏。

（艾德加下。）

（在葛勞塞斯特城堡的一個房間。康沃爾、里根、貢納莉、艾德蒙與僕
　人們上。）

康沃爾（對貢納莉）：派遣一名信差，帶著這封信去給你的夫君。
　法蘭斯的軍隊已經登陸，去找葛勞塞斯特那個叛徒！

（幾名僕人下。）

里根：當場絞死他！

貢納莉：挖出他的眼珠子！

康沃爾：將他交予我處置吧。艾德蒙，留下來陪伴貢納莉，我
　們針對你那叛國的父親所計畫的復仇行動，不適合讓你親
　眼目睹。待你見到公爵時請轉告他備戰，我們亦會作好準
　備。（奧斯華上。）國王何在？

奧斯華：葛勞塞斯特閣下已將他帶走。他約有三十名左右的
　騎士，以及葛勞塞斯特閣下的幾名手下，在城門口與他會
　合，他們已悉數前往多佛，稱在那兒有武裝齊備的朋友
　們。

康沃爾：去為你家夫人備馬。

貢納莉：再會了，我親愛的夫君和妹妹。

康沃爾：艾德蒙，再會。（貢納莉、艾德蒙與奧斯華下。）去找那個
　叛徒葛勞塞斯特，將他當作竊賊似地捆綁，帶他來見我們。
　　（其他僕人們下。）雖然未經審判不得處死他，但是我們能發
　洩怒氣。憤怒可以歸咎，但是不能遏制。來者何人？是那個
　叛徒嗎？

（僕人們上，帶著他們的俘虜葛勞塞斯特。）

里根：那忘恩負義的老狐狸！他來了！

康沃爾：綁緊他那萎縮的雙臂！

葛勞塞斯特：閣下所謂何意？我的好友們，別忘了你們是我的賓客。莫要傷害我，朋友們。

康沃爾：我說捆綁他！

（僕人們將他捆綁。）

里根：綁緊！綁緊！喔，你這齷齪的叛徒！

葛勞塞斯特：無情的夫人啊，我不是！

康沃爾：將他綁在這張椅子上。你近日曾收到法蘭斯的什麼來信？

里根：直接回答，因我們已知曉真相。

葛勞塞斯特：我從中立來源收到一封內容含糊的信件，並非來自敵營。

康沃爾：你將國王送往何處？

葛勞塞斯特：送去多佛了。

里根：何以送去多佛？

葛勞塞斯特：我不能眼睜睜看著你殘酷的指甲挖除他可憐的老眼珠子，或是你姊姊的殘忍毒牙劃破他神聖的血肉。可憐年邁的他承受了此般的暴風雨，助長了眾神的憤怒。倘若當時是野狼在你的門口嗥叫，你也會說：「讓牠們進來。」其他所有殘酷無情的動物們尚且有惻隱之心，但是我將看到如你們這般的不孝子女受到上天的報復。

康沃爾：你永遠也看不到。（對僕人們：）你們抓住那張椅子，我要踩爛你的那雙眼睛！

（葛勞塞斯特被壓制在他坐的椅子上，同時康沃爾用腳踩瞎了他的一隻眼睛。）

葛勞塞斯特：救命！喔，殘忍啊！喔，眾神啊！

里根：剩下的一隻眼睛會嘲笑另一隻眼睛，將他的另一隻眼睛也踩瞎吧！

僕人一：住手，老爺！我自小便服侍你至今，但是我對你最好的服侍莫過於此刻阻止你動手！

里根：胡說，你這隻狗！

康沃爾：你這惡徒！

（他拔劍揮向僕人。）

僕人一：那好吧，放馬過來！儘管向憤怒之人挑戰吧！

（他拔劍，他們打鬥，康沃爾受了傷。）

里根（對另一名僕人）：把你的劍給我。大膽刁民，竟敢如此犯上？

（她從背後用劍刺穿了那名僕人。）

僕人一：喔，我完了！老爺，你還剩下一隻眼睛，能看到他得到報應！喔！

（他死去。）

康沃爾：為免它再多看，我要一勞永逸。（他挖出葛勞塞斯特的另一隻眼睛。）出來吧，你這邪惡的膠狀物！如今你的光彩何在？

葛勞塞斯特：一切盡是黑暗與苦悶孤寂。我的兒子何在？艾德蒙！召喚所有自然的光芒，報復這駭人的暴行吧！

里根：滾出去，你這叛逆的惡徒！你召喚的是憎恨你之人，就是他來向我們告發你的謀逆罪行。

葛勞塞斯特：喔，我真是愚昧！艾德加被冤枉了。仁慈的眾神，請原諒我吧！

里根（對一名僕人）：將他逐出大門外，讓他一路靠嗅覺前往多佛。（對康沃爾：）你可安好，我的夫君？

康沃爾：我受傷了。隨我來，夫人。將那個無眼惡徒逐出去。順便將他那已亡故的僕人扔到糞堆。里根，我大量失血，這傷口來得不是時候。把你的臂膀借給我。

（康沃爾下，由里根攙扶著他。僕人們為葛勞塞斯特鬆綁，帶他離開。其他僕人們抬著死亡的僕人出去。）

僕人二：倘若她能長命百歲，最後壽終正寢，那所有的女人都將變成野獸！

僕人三：讓我們跟著老公爵，他想去哪兒就讓那個瘋子領著他去吧。瘋子做的事沒人會質疑。

僕人二：你去吧，我去取些藥物來為他臉上的傷止血。如今他只能聽天由命！

（他們分別從不同的方向下。）

第四幕

● 第一場　　　　　　　　　　　　　　　　　　　　　　　P. 085

（荒野；艾德加上，仍然偽裝成一個瘋子。）

艾德加：如此甚好──遭人公然蔑視──好過被人私下鄙棄，又被諂媚之言蒙騙。然而，在一切陷入谷底之際，情勢只能轉好。來者何人？（葛勞塞斯特上，由一名老人引領。）我的父親，被一介平民領著？世界啊，喔，世界！是對你詭變的憎恨幫助我們接納死亡。

老人（對葛勞塞斯特）：喔，我的好閣下，我在你的土地上居住了八十載。

葛勞塞斯特：快走！好朋友，你走吧，你的幫助對我毫無裨益，還可能對你有害。

老人：你眼盲看不見前路。

葛勞塞斯特：我已無去路，所以不需要雙眼。我在看得見時亦跌跌蹌蹌；我們的不幸經常是塞翁失馬。喔，我親愛的兒子艾德加，你成了愚蠢的父親盛怒之下的犧牲品！倘若我能活著再遇上你，即便用雙手觸碰你，亦無異於重獲雙眼的視力啊！

老人（注意到艾德加）：是發瘋的窮酸湯姆，那個乞丐。

葛勞塞斯特：他想必尚有點理智，否則就不可能乞討了。

艾德加（竊語）：我的父親是怎麼了？（大聲說：）祝福你，先生！

葛勞塞斯特：這可就是那個瘋子？

老人：他是乞丐，也是瘋子，閣下。

葛勞塞斯特：那就請你走吧，為了你自身的安全。我請這位先生引領我的去路。

老人：哎呀，先生，他是瘋子啊。

葛勞塞斯特：當瘋子引領盲人前行之時，此乃時局紊亂病態之徵兆。照我的話去做，你走吧！

（老人下。）

葛勞塞斯特：這位先生！你好！

艾德加：窮酸湯姆好冷啊。（竊語：）我無法再偽裝下去，但是我不得不這麼做！（大聲說：）願上天庇佑你的雙眼，它們流血了。

葛勞塞斯特：你可知道如何前往多佛？

艾德加：我知道，先生。

葛勞塞斯特：有一座懸崖，高聳得令人俯瞰底下的海浪拍岸，會不禁心生畏懼。帶我去那個懸崖邊，我會給你重賞。到那兒之後我就不需要有人領路了。

艾德加：這是我的手臂，窮酸湯姆這就為你領路。

（他們下。）

P. 088

● **第二場**

（在阿爾邦尼公爵的宮殿附近；貢納莉與艾德蒙上，兩人一同從葛勞塞斯特的城堡返回。）

貢納莉：歡迎你，閣下，我很訝異我的夫君竟未趕在途中迎接我們。（奧斯華上。）你家老爺何在？

奧斯華：在屋內，夫人，但是沒見過有人如此性情大變。我告知他軍隊已然登陸，他一笑置之；當我向他提及你將返回之時，他說：「那就更不妙了。」然後我告訴他葛勞塞斯特的叛逆情事，以及他兒子的忠誠效命，他竟罵我是個白癡，還說我此言是在顛倒是非！

貢納莉（對艾德蒙）：你先回去吧，他太過於懦弱而不敢採取任何行動。回去吧，艾德蒙，去找我的妹婿，帶領他的軍隊。我要變換在家中的角色了，讓我的夫君做點針線活兒！（**指向奧斯華**。）就讓這個可靠的忠僕當你的中間人吧，你可能未幾即將聽聞——倘若你為自身利益而行動——你家夫人發號施令予你。（**她親吻他**。）這一吻若能開口言語，應能大為提振你的士氣。你知我心意，再會了。

艾德蒙：我將永生效忠於你，至死方休！

貢納莉：我最親愛的艾德蒙！（**艾德蒙下**。）喔，人與人之間的差別竟如此之大！你理應得到一個女人全心全意的付出，而我竟嫁了一個傻瓜。

奧斯華：夫人，我家老爺來了。

（**奧斯華下，阿爾邦尼上**。）

貢納莉：前來迎接我難道不值得嗎？

阿爾邦尼：喔，貢納莉！你就連狂風吹打在你臉上的沙塵都不值得啊！你的性格令我生畏，膽敢忤逆雙親的天性是無法自制的。

貢納莉：莫再多言，你的此番說教皆是謬論。

阿爾邦尼：在邪惡之人的眼中，智慧與良善亦看似邪惡；對於骯髒齷齪之人，骯髒齷齪亦有吸引人之處。你已將你仁厚寬大的父親逼瘋，我的連襟如何能容許此事的發生？

貢納莉：懦夫！眾人皆對你頤指氣使。你的兵符戰令何在？法王在我們的平靜國度搖旗揮兵，戰爭的威脅從四面八方包圍我們——而你這滿口仁義道德的傻瓜，還坐在這兒哭喊著：「他為何這麼做？」

阿爾邦尼：瞧瞧你的真面目吧—你是個惡魔！蛇蠍心腸的女人更教人害怕。

貢納莉：你這無用的傻瓜！

阿爾邦尼：可恥啊！莫要有野獸般一般的行徑！倘若我讓我的雙手依循著我的情感行事，此刻必定將你碎屍萬段；但是你有女人的形體在保護著你。

貢納莉（冷笑）：你和你所謂的男子氣概！

（一名信差上。）

第四幕
第二場

阿爾邦尼：你捎來什麼信息？

信差：喔，我的好閣下，康沃爾公爵已死！他在挖出葛勞塞斯特的另一隻眼睛時，被他的僕人用劍殺死。

阿爾邦尼：葛勞塞斯特的眼睛！

信差：一名情緒激動的僕人為了捍衛他，舉劍揮向他偉大的主人；公爵在盛怒之下攻擊他，該名僕人應聲倒地死去——但是他在臨死前給了公爵致命的一擊，致使他在事後傷重身亡。（對貢納莉：）這是令妹給你的書信，夫人。

貢納莉（竊語）：如今她已守寡，而我的艾德蒙此刻就在她的身旁，我對未來的憧憬可能化為泡影。（大聲說。）待我閱畢之後再行回覆。

（貢納莉下。）

阿爾邦尼：當他被挖去雙眼之時，他的兒子何在？

信差：正在和我家夫人趕往此處的途中。

阿爾邦尼：他不在此處。

信差：是的，閣下，我在他回程時巧遇了他。

阿爾邦尼：他可知道此一邪惡行徑？

信差：是的，我的好閣下，就是他告發他父親的罪行。他是蓄意離家的，好讓他們恣意地懲罰他。

阿爾邦尼：葛勞塞斯特，我活著是為了感謝你對國王的忠愛——也是為了報復你被挖去雙眼！（對信差：）過來，朋友，將你所知的一切告知予我。

（他們下。）

●第三場 —————————————————— P. 093

（位於多佛附近的法軍軍營；肯特與一名紳士上。）

肯特：法王何以如此匆忙離去？

紳士：他想起了一件他在自己的王國忘了做的事。

肯特：他臨行前交代哪位將領負責帶兵？

紳士：法蘭斯元帥。

肯特：你的幾封信是否感動考狄利婭而透露出幾許哀傷？

紳士：是的，閣下，她在讀信時淚水從白皙的雙頰滴落。她有一、兩度屏息喊出：「父親！」彷彿那是重壓在她心頭的大石。她哭喊：「兩位姊姊啊！所有女人之恥辱！什麼——在暴風雨中？令人難以置信！」然後她從美麗的雙眸迸發了神聖的淚水。

肯特：是繁星，是我們頭頂上的繁星決定了我們的性格！否則父母是不可能生出如此不同之子女。你後來有再與她交談嗎？

紳士：沒有。

肯特：這是在國王返回法蘭斯之前？

紳士：不，是之後。

肯特：可憐又苦惱的李爾來了。偶爾在他較為清醒之時，他知道我們因何來此，但他拒絕與考狄利婭相會。

紳士：何以如此？

肯特：強烈的羞恥感令他卻步，他想起自己從前對她的冷酷無情。

紳士：哎呀，可憐的陛下！

肯特：你是否聽聞阿爾邦尼和康沃爾軍隊的情況？

紳士：他們正在行軍。

肯特：閣下，我這就帶你去見李爾王陛下，讓你好好照顧他，我目前暫時有要務纏身。等我恢復了真正的身分，你必不會後悔與我有所牽連。請吧，隨我來。

（他們下。）

● 第四場 ———————————— P. 095

（在法蘭斯軍營的一座營帳；考狄利婭、一名醫生與士兵們上。）

考狄利婭：哎呀，是他，有人方才看到他如同波濤洶湧的大海一般瘋狂，高聲地唱著歌，他頭上戴著蘆葦編織的王冠。去找他，帶他來找我們。（**一名軍官下。**）能治好他之人，必能擁有我所有的財產。

醫生：是有個方法，夫人。他缺乏的是睡眠，睡眠即是自然給我們最好的療法，有許多草藥能使他在苦悶之餘闔上眼睛。

考狄利婭：我願以我的淚水，澆灌世間所有能治病的草藥！

（一名信差上。）

信差：英格蘭軍隊即將到來。

考狄利婭：知道了，我們會恭候他們的大駕。喔，親愛的父親！我們是為了你的利益而戰，我的夫君法王憐憫我哀傷的淚水。我們的動機並非出於野心，而是為了愛，為了保衛年邁父親的權益。但願我未幾即能聽聞他的音訊和見到他！

（全體下。）

● 第五場 ———————————— P. 097

（葛勞塞斯特城堡中的一個房間；里根與奧斯華上。）

里根：我姐夫的軍隊是否已經出發？

奧斯華：是的，夫人。

里根：他也隨軍啟程嗎？

奧斯華：夫人，幾經紛擾之後，令姊更像個熟練的軍人。

里根：艾德蒙閣下是否在他府上與你家老爺相談？

奧斯華：沒有，夫人。

里根：為何家姐書信予他？

奧斯華：我不知道，夫人。

里根：是啊，他確實是有要事在身而外出。在我們弄瞎了葛勞塞斯特的雙眼之後，還留他活口著實為不智之舉。無論他前往何處，他必會慫恿眾人與我們為敵。我想艾德蒙應該是去結束他父親悲慘的一生了，出於對他不幸遭遇的同情，再者，他亦有意一探敵軍的虛實。

奧斯華：我必須帶著此信前去找他，我家夫人嚴令要我不辱使命。

里根：她為何要寫信給艾德蒙？你難道不能代傳她的口信嗎？或許──我不知道──就當是我欠你一份人情──讓我拆信詳閱吧。

奧斯華：夫人，我還是──

里根：我知道她並不愛她的丈夫，這點我很確定。當她日前來到此地時，她對艾德蒙閣下頻送秋波，不時以眼神傳情示意。我知道你和她關係匪淺，所以請你聽好：我找艾德蒙談過了，他對我比對你家夫人更感興趣。你應該明白我的意思，將此信交予他。（她遞給奧斯華一封信。）當你將我所說的每一句話告訴你家夫人時，請你勸她三思而後行。那就再會吧，倘若你碰巧聽聞那個瞎眼叛徒的信息，但凡了結他性命之人必得拔擢晉升。

奧斯華：但願我能遇見他，夫人！我會證明我的忠誠向於何人。

里根：再會了。

（兩人下。）

●第六場

（多佛附近的鄉間；葛勞塞斯特上，由艾德加領路。）

葛勞塞斯特：到那個山頭還要多遠？

艾德加：你已正在攀登這座山。

葛勞塞斯特：我覺得地面似乎是平坦的。

艾德加：山坡非常陡，你是否聽到海浪聲？

葛勞塞斯特：我沒聽到，而且我覺得你的聲音變了，你說話比起從前要清晰得多。

艾德加：你錯了，我仍是一樣。

葛勞塞斯特：不，我覺得你比從前更善於言詞。

艾德加：來吧，先生，正是此地，我們稍作停留。（他們在一片原野上，但是艾德加假裝那是一座懸崖。）低頭俯視令我頭暈目眩！走在海灘上的漁民，看似老鼠一般渺小。我不再看了，免得我頭昏眼花，視線模糊可能使我跟蹌摔落懸崖。

葛勞塞斯特：帶我到你所站立之處。

艾德加：把你的手給我，你正站在懸崖邊緣不遠之處。

葛勞塞斯特：放開我的手。來，朋友，這是另一個錢袋，內有珍貴的珠寶，但願幸運之神能助你享用之！就此別過，讓我聽見你離開的聲音。

艾德加（假裝要走）：再見了，閣下。（竊語：）我此般戲弄他的絕望，純粹是為了治癒他。

葛勞塞斯特（跪下）：喔，偉大的眾神！我將捨棄這世界和我莫大的痛苦。倘若我能繼續咬牙苦忍，我會忍耐。倘若艾德加尚在人間，喔，祝福他！（對艾德加：）好了，朋友，再會了！（他俯身向前，彷彿跳下懸崖一般。）

艾德加（假裝在遠處）：我走了，先生，再會。（現在假裝成懸崖下的一名漁夫：）嗨，先生！朋友！你聽得見嗎？說話啊！你是何人，先生？

葛勞塞斯特：走開，讓我死。

艾德加：你從超過十艘船的桅杆高度之處摔落！還活著可謂是奇蹟！

葛勞塞斯特：我究竟有否摔落？

艾德加：有的——從這白堊懸崖的頂端摔落而下。你看看那上面，抬頭看看！

葛勞塞斯特：哎呀，我已無眼可看。

艾德加：把你的手臂給我，我來扶你上去。你可無恙？雙腿還有感覺嗎？顯然是眾神救了你的性命。

葛勞塞斯特：從今爾後，我會忍耐苦痛，直到命運決定我此生已足矣——然後我會死去。

艾德加：要有耐心。來者何人？（李爾上，怪異地全身綴滿鮮花。）神志清醒之人不可能作此打扮。真是令人心碎的景象啊！

李爾：你看，你看，有老鼠！來，用這片烤過的起司就能捉住牠了。（他撕碎假想的一塊起司，扔在地上，然後跟隨著假想的一支飛箭往前行。）喔，飛得真好啊，鳥兒！一箭命中！（看到艾德加：）說出通關密語。

艾德加：甜美的馬鬱蘭。

李爾：你可以通過了。

葛勞塞斯特：我認識你，你可是國王陛下？

李爾：是的，如假包換的國王！

葛勞塞斯特：喔，讓我親吻你的手！

李爾：待朕先將手擦乾淨，手上有死亡的臭味。

葛勞塞斯特：喔，此人已心神全毀！你認識我嗎？

李爾：你那雙眼睛朕記得一清二楚。你可是在斜睨朕？

葛勞塞斯特：怎麼，用我無眼的黑洞？

李爾：喔，你是在玩遊戲嗎？你頭上沒有眼睛，真令人感到悲哀，但你也知道這世界本是如此。

葛勞塞斯特：我是憑感覺在看的。

李爾：怎麼，你瘋了嗎？無眼之人亦可看清世事，用你的耳朵吧。倘若你要為朕的不幸而啜泣，就取走朕的雙眼。朕知道你是何人，你是葛勞塞斯特，但聽朕的諄諄告誡──聽啊！

葛勞塞斯特：哎呀，可嘆的一天！

李爾：嬰孩在出生之際，即因降臨這充滿傻瓜的偌大舞台而哭泣。（他在瘋癲之餘，思緒紊亂不堪。）用毛氈為一群戰馬上蹄鐵，不失為一個好主意，朕必須試試，待朕躡足潛近那兩個女婿，朕就要殺、殺、殺、殺！

（一名紳士上，帶著侍從們。）

紳士：喔，他在這兒，捉住他。

李爾：朕是國王，你可知否？

紳士：你是國王陛下，我們服從你。

李爾：那就還有希望。來吧，倘若你有此意，就得趕緊追上來！

（他逃跑，侍從們緊追而上。）

紳士：即使是最卑賤之人也是令人同情的景象，更何況是國王，簡直令人無法言喻！

艾德加：你是否聽聞即將生起戰事？

紳士：那當然，眾人皆已聞之。

艾德加：敵軍距離我們多近？

紳士：非常近，而且迅速逼近中。

艾德加：謝謝你，先生，沒別的事了。

（紳士下。）

葛勞塞斯特：這位好先生，你是何人？

艾德加：一個極其貧窮之人，因遭逢不幸而破產。把你的手給我，我來領你前去避難之處。

葛勞塞斯特：由衷地感謝你。

（奧斯華上，他看到葛勞塞斯特。）

奧斯華：那是被通緝懸賞之人！令人開心的一天！你無眼的頭顱將使我致富！（他拔劍。）你這不快樂的老叛徒，劍已出鞘將取你性命。

葛勞塞斯特(準備受死)**：**但願你友善的手有足夠的氣力殺死我。

（艾德加挺身向前捍衛他的父親。）

奧斯華：你這大膽刁民，竟敢捍衛一個叛國的不法之徒？放開他的手臂。

艾德加：沒有更好的理由，先生，我是不會放手的。

奧斯華：放手，無恥之徒，否則要你陪葬！

艾德加：倘若有人能騙取我的性命，那我幾星期前便已一命嗚呼。來吧！我不害怕你的劍！

（他們打鬥，艾德加傷了他。奧斯華倒地。）

奧斯華：無恥之徒，你殺了我！惡徒，取走我的錢袋吧。倘若你曾有過平步青雲的祈望，燒了我的遺體吧，將我隨身帶的書信交給葛勞塞斯特伯爵艾德蒙，你在英格蘭軍隊即可找到他。喔，壯志未酬身先死！（他死了。）

艾德加：我甚是瞭解你，你是名副其實的惡徒，甘願效忠於你家夫人助紂為虐。

葛勞塞斯特：怎麼──他死了嗎？

艾德加：坐吧，好先生，稍作休息，我們來瞧瞧他在口袋裡放了什麼，他提到的書信或許能有所助益。（他找到那封信，拆開封蠟。）真是抱歉了，高尚的封蠟，莫要說我是不懂禮數，欲知敵人的心意，只得扒開他們的心！撕開他們的書信才是較為合法之舉。（他讀信。）記住你我共有的誓言，你會有許多機會殺死他。倘若他凱旋歸來，我們就會一無所成，屆時我將成為他的俘虜，他的床榻將是我的囚牢。請你拯救我免於落入此般命運，向我證明你對我的愛。你的妻子（此乃我心所願）和深愛你的奴僕，貢納莉。喔，最毒婦人心！竟然密謀殺害她高尚的丈夫，讓我弟弟取而代之！（對奧斯華：）我要將此封惡毒的書信交予公爵，務必將你的死訊和你邪惡的勾當告訴他。

（艾德加下，拖著奧斯華的屍體。）

葛勞塞斯特：國王已經發瘋，而我的心志竟是如此固執，堅持保持清醒來體驗我至深的悲痛！不如讓我也發瘋，使我忘卻那些惱人的傷痛。

（從遠處傳來鼓聲。）

艾德加：來吧，我要將你交託給一位朋友。

（兩人下。）

●第七場 ————————————— P. 107

（法蘭斯軍營的一座營帳；李爾躺在床上熟睡；音樂聲響起；醫生、紳士與其他人在照顧李爾；考狄利婭與肯特上。）

考狄利婭：喔，好肯特！我如何才能報答你的好意？

肯特：能得到你的感激，夫人，我已是受之有愧。

考狄利婭：去更衣吧，那身衣服使人想起不堪的過去。

肯特：夫人，現在被認出來實在有違我的計畫，請你在時機成熟之前假裝不認識我。

考狄利婭：那就依你吧，我的好閣下。（對醫生：）國王的情況如何？

醫生：夫人，他仍在熟睡中，能否允許我們喚醒他？他已經睡了很久。

考狄利婭：做你認為最妥當的事吧。

醫生：在我們喚醒他之時，夫人，請你務必在此，我相信他會很正常的。

考狄利婭：好的。（對李爾：）喔，親愛的父親！但願我的雙唇能治好你，讓這一吻修復我的兩個姊姊對你造成的重創吧！

（她親吻他的額頭。）

肯特：善良又可愛的公主！

考狄利婭：即便你不是她們的父親，你的白髮亦值得憐憫。這就是迎擊暴風雨的那張臉嗎？抵禦最駭人的雷電？屹立在可怕的閃電之中？徹夜難眠——可憐的迷失的靈魂——這個只有稀疏毛髮的頭頂？我敵人的狗，縱使牠咬了我，那樣的夜晚我亦會邀牠到我的火堆前取暖。哎呀，哎呀！沒想到你的生命和神智竟不是同時結束的。他醒了，快和他說話。

醫生：夫人，你來說吧，這樣最好。

考狄利婭（對李爾）：我的國王陛下可安好？

李爾：你從墳墓中救出了朕，才是害了朕啊。你是幸福之人，而我卻身陷苦難之中，被捆綁在火輪上，被自己的淚水像融化的鉛般燒灼。

考狄利婭：陛下，你認得我嗎？

李爾：你是亡靈，朕知道。你是何時死亡的？

考狄利婭（對醫生）：他仍是神志不清。

醫生：他才剛醒過來。

李爾：朕去了哪裡？這是何處？

考狄利婭：給我你的祝福吧，陛下。（*李爾看了她一眼，然後跪倒在她的腳邊。*）不，陛下，你不能下跪！

李爾：請你莫要取笑朕，朕是個愚蠢至極的老頭，已經八十多歲了，而且説句實在話，恐怕朕的神志不甚清楚。朕應該認識你，也認得這個人，但是朕心存疑惑，甚至不記得自己昨晚睡在何處。切莫嘲笑朕，這位夫人應該是朕的孩子考狄利婭。

考狄利婭：我真的是啊，我是。

李爾：你的淚水是濕的嗎？是的，莫再哭泣。倘若你有毒藥給朕，朕必定一飲而盡。朕知道你不愛朕；在朕的記憶中，你的兩位姊姊虐待了朕。你有理由殺死朕，她們沒有。

考狄利婭（*啜泣*）：沒有理由，沒有理由。

醫生：請你寬慰，夫人，他這瘋病症狀已然緩解，但是填補他記憶中的空缺仍屬危險，在他更平靜之前莫要再驚擾他。

考狄利婭：陛下想去散步嗎？

李爾：你必須耐心待朕，現在要請你忘記和原諒，朕已老邁又糊塗。

（*李爾、考狄利婭、醫生與侍從們下。*）

紳士：康沃爾果真就這樣遇害了？

肯特：確實如此，先生。

紳士：現在他的部屬是聽誰的號令？

肯特：據説是葛勞塞斯特的私生子。

紳士：聽聞他那被放逐的兒子艾德加，此刻正在日耳曼和肯特伯爵在一起。

肯特：眾說紛紜，我們必須先行準備，王國的軍隊很快就會到來。

紳士：此場戰役很可能是腥風血雨。再會了，先生。

（紳士下。）

肯特：我的生死取決於今日之戰事。

（肯特下。）

第五幕

● 第一場 ————————————————— P. 113

（英軍在多佛附近的軍營；艾德蒙、里根、軍官們、士兵們與其他人上。）

里根：好了，親愛的閣下，請你老實告訴我，你真的不愛我姊姊嗎？

艾德蒙：此心可昭日月。

里根：你是否曾與她有過親密行為？

艾德蒙：沒有，我以名譽起誓，夫人。

里根：我決不可能容忍她，閣下，切莫與她太過親密。

艾德蒙：莫要擔心。（鼓聲響起。）她來了，與她的夫君同行！

（阿爾邦尼、貢納莉與士兵們上。）

貢納莉（竊語）：我寧可戰敗，也不願讓我妹妹介入他和我之間。

阿爾邦尼（向里根行禮）：你好，親愛的妹妹。（對艾德蒙：）先生，此乃我之所聞：國王已至他女兒的住處，因我們的嚴刑峻

法而不得不出走的其他人亦隨之同往。我向來不好征戰，我們只是因為法蘭斯的入侵而迫於無奈。

里根：你又何需多言？

貢納莉：團結一致抵禦敵人，此時不宜爭辯這些家務事。

阿爾邦尼：問問專家們該如何是好。

艾德蒙：我們將盡快去你的營帳找你商議。

（在眾人皆尚未離開之前，偽裝的艾德加上。）

艾德加（對阿爾邦尼）：能否借一步說話？

阿爾邦尼（對其他人）：你們先去，我隨後就到。（全體下，獨留阿爾邦尼與艾德加。）（對艾德加：）說吧。

艾德加：在兩軍交戰之前，先拆開這封信。倘若你戰勝，就讓號角聲響起；雖然我看似卑微，但是我能化身為勝利的鬥士，證明我此刻之所言無半點虛假。倘若你戰敗，你什麼也不必管，一切就此了結。祝你好運！

阿爾邦尼：留下來等我看完信再走。

艾德加：恕我難以從命。待時機成熟之時，吹響勝利的號角吧，我會再次出現的。

阿爾邦尼：那就再會了，我會詳讀你的信。

（艾德加下。艾德蒙再上。）

艾德蒙：敵軍已現蹤跡。召集你的軍隊吧，快點行動。

阿爾邦尼：我們會竭盡全力的。

（阿爾邦尼下。）

艾德蒙：我對那兩姐妹皆已海誓山盟地示愛，兩人各自懷疑對方，我該接受何人才好？兩個都要？要一個？還是都不要？倘若姊妹倆都活著，就誰也過不上好日子了。接受那個寡婦將激怒她的姊姊貢納莉，但是貢納莉的丈夫還活著，我難以實現我的計畫，所以暫時利用他來作戰吧，等待戰爭結束之後，再讓一心想除掉親夫的她來決定。至於他想對李爾和考狄利婭手下留情，待戰爭結束、他們成了我們的俘虜之後，他們絕對得不到寬恕。唯有起而行才對我最有利，而非坐而空言。

（艾德蒙下。）

● 第二場———————————————————— P. 116

（在兩軍陣營之間的原野上；李爾與考狄利婭帶著部分軍隊走過舞台之後下，接著艾德加與葛勞塞斯特上。）

艾德加：好先生，在這棵樹下休息吧，祈求正義的一方戰勝。倘若我能回來，我會帶給你撫慰人心的消息。

葛勞塞斯特：願神的恩典與你同在，先生！

（艾德加下。戰爭的聲響愈來愈大，聽到了撤退聲。艾德加再上，驚慌失措。）

艾德加：快走吧，老先生！李爾王已戰敗，他和他的女兒雙雙被俘虜。把你的手給我，快走！

（他們下。）

● 第三場 P. 117

（英軍在多佛附近的軍營；艾德蒙上，帶著李爾與考狄利婭兩名戰俘，有士兵們在看守他們。）

艾德蒙：嚴加看守他們，直到我們知悉主事者們意欲如何處置他們。

考狄利婭（對李爾）：因善意而蒙受最大的苦難者，我們並非第一人。

李爾：讓我們前去監牢吧，我們兩人要像籠中鳥一般獨自鳴唱。當你要求朕祝福你之時，朕會跪地懇求你的原諒，所以我們要活著禱告和歌唱，傳述古老的故事，嘲笑身著華服的朝臣。

艾德蒙：把他們帶走。

李爾：既使眾神也會為你這般犧牲祈禱，考狄利婭。（她哭泣。）莫要哭泣，如今我們再也不會分開。擦乾你的淚水，他們在使我們啜泣之前會先腐朽敗壞。來吧！

（在守衛的隨同之下，李爾與考狄利婭下。）

艾德蒙（對一名軍官）：過來，隊長，帶著這張字條，跟隨他們前往監牢。服從這上面的指示，我必有重賞。聽好了：識時務者為俊傑，從軍之人不能心軟；你若不答應聽命行事，就另覓他法以求飛黃騰達吧。

隊長：我不能像馬匹似地拉車；倘若這是人的工作，我必定照辦。

（他下。號角聲響起。阿爾邦尼、貢納莉、里根、軍官們與侍從們上。）

阿爾邦尼（對艾德蒙）：我命令今日作戰所得之戰俘──要得到他們應受的待遇。

艾德蒙：閣下，我認為最好讓他們在戒護之下遠離此地。國王的年齡和頭銜，可能動搖百姓的情緒──使我方的將士起而造反。明天，或稍晚，才是審判他們的較好時機。

阿爾邦尼：閣下稍安勿躁，我在此一戰役中視你為臣民──而非與我平起平坐。

里根（對阿爾邦尼）：他帶領我們的軍隊，在我的授權之下行事，這就足以讓他的位階與你齊平了。

貢納莉：且慢，他是憑藉自身的實力而位居高階，而非因你的相助。

里根：他以我之名、在我的授意下行事，才最是與他齊平。

貢納莉：除非他娶你為妻，否則未有此等可能。

里根：弄臣往往才是真正的先知。

貢納莉（諷刺地）：好啊、好啊、好啊。

里根：夫人，我可一點也不好，否則我會痛斥你一頓。（對艾德蒙：）將軍，帶著我的士兵們、我的俘虜們和我繼承的家產，隨你如何處置，我亦悉聽尊便。願世人見證我在此使你成為我的夫君和一家之主。

貢納莉：你是打算委身於他？

阿爾邦尼（對貢納莉，生氣地）：此事由不得你！

艾德蒙：也由不得你，閣下。

阿爾邦尼：確實如此！

里根（對艾德蒙）：讓鼓聲響起，宣告屬於我的一切皆為你所有。

阿爾邦尼：且慢，聽我的勸說！艾德蒙，我要以叛亂之名逮捕你，還有你的共犯（指向貢納莉。），這貼了金箔的毒蛇！

貢納莉：一派胡言！

阿爾邦尼：你身懷武器，艾德蒙。讓號角聲響起吧，倘若無人前來以打鬥證明你的多條叛逆罪，那我便親自上場！這是我的挑戰！

（他扔下了一隻手套。）

里根：不好，喔，我身體不適！

貢納莉（竊語）：倘若你未有不適，我就再也不相信毒藥了。

艾德蒙（扔下一隻手套）：此乃我的回應！稱我為叛徒之人，乃像個惡徒似地滿口謊言！但凡膽敢趨前之人，我會誓死捍衛我的名譽，對付他、你或其他任何人！

阿爾邦尼（叫喊）：傳令官，過來！

里根（搖搖欲墜）：我的身體愈來愈不適。

阿爾邦尼：她不舒服，帶她去我的營帳。（里根下，由軍官們攙扶。一名傳令官上。）過來，傳令官，吹響號角，宣讀此書。（他將艾德蒙的挑戰書交予他。）

（傳令官吹響號角。）

傳令官（宣讀內容）：「倘若軍隊中有任何位階或殊勳之人，指稱葛勞塞斯特伯爵艾德蒙是叛徒，就讓他在第三聲號角響起之前現身，他會大膽地捍衛自己。」

（號角聲三響，中間各有停頓，然後艾德加在更多號角聲宣示之後步上前來。）

201

傳令官：應號角聲前來者是何人？

艾德加：我的姓名並未登記在冊，早已被叛亂罪毀壞殆盡，但是我和我意欲決鬥的對象是同等地尊貴。

阿爾邦尼：那是何人？

艾德加：誰要為葛勞塞斯特伯爵艾德蒙而戰？

艾德蒙（上前）：就是他本人，你有何話要對他說？

艾德加：拔劍吧，這是我的劍！你是個叛徒，背叛了你的眾神、你的兄弟和你的父親。倘若你否認，這把劍、這條臂膀和我最大的勇氣必將證明你在撒謊！

艾德蒙：依據騎士團的規則，我可以延後這場比鬥，但是我拒絕這麼做，我要將你的叛逆指控拋回給你，再加上可憎的撒謊罪名。我都要用這把劍為它們開路，讓它們永遠留在那兒。號角聲，響啊！

（號角聲響起。艾德蒙與艾德加決鬥，艾德蒙重傷倒地。）

阿爾邦尼：救他，快救他！

貢納莉：這是詭計，艾德蒙。依據比鬥慣例，你毋須與不認識的對手比試。你並未戰敗，而是被矇騙和欺詐。

阿爾邦尼：閉上你的嘴，女人，否則我會用這張紙塞住它！（那是貢納莉寫給艾德蒙的書信，是艾德加於第四幕第六場在奧斯華身上發現的。）（對艾德加：）握好你的劍，先生。（對貢納莉：）你簡直惡毒到難以言喻！我猜想你應該知道此為何物。

（艾德蒙接下這封書信。）

貢納莉：是又如何？我是女王，律法是為我所有，而不是你；誰能以此而起訴我？

阿爾邦尼：禽獸！你知道這封信嗎？

貢納莉：莫要問我知道什麼。

（貢納莉下，惱羞成怒。）

阿爾邦尼（對一名軍官）：追上去，她已陷入絕望境地，妥善照看她。

（軍官下。）

艾德蒙（對阿爾邦尼）：你對我的指控並無虛假——還有更多，罄竹難書，早晚是紙包不住火。一切皆已結束，我也完了。
（對艾德加：）但你究竟是誰，這擊敗我之人究竟是何身分？倘若你是貴族，我就原諒你。

艾德加：我和你是同等的貴族身分，艾德蒙。我名喚艾德加，我是你父親的兒子。眾神是公正的，祂們用我們所耽溺的罪行當作懲罰我們的手段。賦與你生命讓他失去了雙眼。

艾德蒙：你方才所言不假，確為事實。

阿爾邦尼（對艾德加）：我從你走路的姿態即看出你必是貴族身分。歡迎你，倘若我曾憎惡你或你的父親，就讓悲傷劈開我的心吧！

艾德加：可敬的公爵，我知你心意。

阿爾邦尼：你這陣子躲哪兒去了？你如何得知你父親遭遇的不幸？

艾德加：因我將之放在心上。且聽我簡短道來：為了逃過加諸在我身上的死劫，我穿著襤褸衣衫，行徑有如瘋癲之人。我穿著這身破衣裳，遇見了我那雙眼被弄瞎、眼窩淌血的父親。我成了他的引導，為他乞討、拯救他於絕望之中。我未曾向他透露我的身分，直到半小時之前我身披鎧甲，請求他保佑我，將我的流浪歷程向他娓娓道來。他備受創傷的心中悲喜參半，滿溢著快樂。

艾德蒙：你此番話語令我感動莫名，或許亦有所裨益。繼續説吧，你看似還有更多話要説。

艾德加：在我咆哮著喊出我的悲傷之際，有個人恰巧經過。當他認出我時，他用強壯的臂膀環抱住我的頸項，彷彿衝破天際似地放聲號哭。接著他擁抱了我的父親，將任何人前所未聞的關於李爾和他自身的悲慘故事告訴了他。在他陳述的同時，他的悲傷之情愈顯強烈，生命的意志力亦搖搖欲墜。然後號角聲響起，我拋下了昏迷的他先行離去。

阿爾邦尼：但那是何人？

艾德加：是肯特，閣下——被驅逐出境的肯特。他偽裝自己，追隨著放逐他的國王，比任何奴隸待他更好。

（一名紳士上，手持一把染血的刀。）

紳士：救命，救命！喔，救命！

艾德加：這把染血的刀是何意？

紳士：這尚且溫熱……還冒著蒸氣……從她的心臟拔出來的……喔！她死了！

阿爾邦尼：誰死了？説啊。

紳士：你的夫人，閣下，你的妻子，她毒害了她的妹妹，她已自白認罪。

艾德蒙：我和她們姐妹倆都訂了親！我們三人未幾即將重聚。

艾德加：肯特來了。

阿爾邦尼：將她們都抬上來，無論死活。我們所敬畏的眾神，祂們的審判是毫不留情的。

（紳士下，肯特上。）

肯特：我是來敬祝國王陛下和公爵閣下永遠地晚安。他不在
　　　這兒嗎？

阿爾邦尼：重大的疏失！說話啊，艾德蒙，國王身在何處？考狄
　　　利婭何在？（貢納莉與里根的遺體被人抬進來。）你是否看到此
　　　一景象，肯特？

肯特：哎呀！出了什麼事？

艾德蒙：所以艾德蒙果真是被愛的！一個為了我毒害了另一
　　　個，然後自我了斷。

阿爾邦尼：確實如此，掩住她們的臉。

艾德蒙：我命不久矣，意欲做些良善之事，儘管我天性本惡。
　　　快去城堡！我已下令在那兒處死李爾和考狄利婭。速速前
　　　去，及時趕去救人。

阿爾邦尼：跑，快跑！喔，快跑！

艾德加：下令給誰，閣下？由誰負責？將你的信物送去，下令暫
　　　緩行刑。

艾德蒙：此法甚好。取我的劍去，交給隊長。

艾德加（將艾德蒙的劍交給一名軍官）：快！務必要快！

（軍官快步跑開。）

艾德蒙（對阿爾邦尼）：他奉了你的妻子和我的命令，要在監牢
　　　裡絞死考狄利婭，謊稱她是在絕望之餘自縊而死。

阿爾邦尼：願眾神庇護她！（對僕人們：）暫時帶他下去。

（艾德蒙被抬走。李爾再上，考狄利婭死在他的懷中。）

李爾：哀嚎、哀嚎、哀嚎、哀嚎！喔，你們是鐵石心腸之人！
　　　她就此一去不復返！

肯特（跪在李爾面前）：喔，我的好陛下！

李爾：走開！

艾德加：此乃高尚的肯特，你的朋友。

李爾：詛咒你們！殺人兇手、叛徒！朕本可救她，如今她已香消玉殞！考狄利婭、考狄利婭！再多留一會兒！（他用耳朵貼近她的嘴唇。）你說什麼？她的聲音曾如此溫婉、輕柔和微弱——此乃女人之美德。朕殺了絞死你的那個惡徒！

軍官：確實如此，諸位閣下，他此言不假。

李爾：可不是嗎？（看到肯特。）你是何人？你不就是肯特嗎？

肯特：正是在下，你的僕人肯特。你的僕人凱厄斯何在？

李爾（認出肯特在偽裝時所用的名字）：他是個好人，這朕可以告訴你！他會打鬥，而且速度甚快。（傷心地。）他死了，屍體已然腐爛。

肯特：不，我的好陛下，從你遭逢不幸之初便跟隨著你悲傷腳步的那人就是我。

李爾（不明白）：歡迎你來到此地。

肯特：一切皆如此淒涼、黯淡而致命，你的長女和次女均陷入絕望之境而自我了結生命。

李爾（仍然不明白）：是的，我想也是。

阿爾邦尼：他已是語無倫次，再和他多說亦是無益。

艾德加：毫無裨益。

（一名軍官上。）

軍官：艾德蒙已死，閣下。

阿爾邦尼：此事已無關緊要。諸位閣下與貴族們，仔細聽我意欲實行之事：我們要竭力安慰這沉淪的高貴之人；至於我們，我們將辭官，將我們的權力轉交給這位年老的陛下，伴他共度餘生。（對艾德加與肯特：）至於你們，你倆將重拾你們的貴族身分，再加上你們高尚的行為所應得之頭銜。所有朋友們的忠誠皆能得到封賞，而所有敵人們亦將受到應有的懲罰。喔，你們看，快看！

李爾：朕可憐的孩子被絞死了！不，不，沒了氣息！何以一條狗、一匹馬、一隻老鼠都有生命，而你卻氣息全無？你將不再回來，再也、再也、再也、再也、再也未有可能！（他拼命拉扯自己的衣領。）請你解開這個鈕扣。謝謝你，先生。你有看到這個嗎？看看她！你看！她的嘴唇！你看那兒，看那兒！

（在極度悲痛之下，他死去。）

艾德加：他昏厥了！（搖晃著李爾。）陛下！

肯特：碎吧，我的心。我懇求你，碎吧！

艾德加（仍在搖晃著李爾）：醒一醒，陛下！

肯特：切莫擾亂他即將脫竅的靈魂，讓他去吧！唯有敵人才會讓他在這無情的世間再多受苦難。

阿爾邦尼：將他們抬走，我們的當務之急是舉國服喪。（對肯特與艾德加：）朋友們，你倆要肩負起這王國的重擔。

艾德加：我們必須挺過這悲傷的時刻。最年長者蒙受了最多的苦難，我們年輕人永遠也看不了那麼多，亦不可能活得那般長久。

（所有的遺體皆被緩步抬走。）

Literary Glossary • 文學詞彙表

aside 竊語

一種台詞。演員在台上講此台詞時,其他角色是聽不見的。角色通常藉由竊語來向觀眾抒發內心感受。

- Although she appeared to be calm, the heroine's **aside** revealed her inner terror.
  雖然女主角看似冷靜,但她的**竊語**透露出她內在的恐懼。

backstage 後台

一個戲院空間。演員都在此處準備上台,舞台布景也存放此處。

- Before entering, the villain impatiently waited **backstage**.
  在上台前,壞人在**後台**焦躁地等待。

cast 演員;卡司陣容

戲劇的全體演出人員。

- The entire **cast** must attend tonight's dress rehearsal.
  全體演員必須參加今晚的正式排練。

character 角色

故事或戲劇中虛構的人物。

- Mighty Mouse is one of my favorite cartoon **characters**.
  太空飛鼠是我最愛的卡通**人物**之一。

climax 劇情高峰

戲劇或小説中主要衝突的結局。

- The outlaw's capture made an exciting **climax** to the story.
  逃犯落網成為故事中最刺激的**精彩情節**。

comedy 喜劇

有趣好笑的戲劇、電影和電視劇，並有快樂完美的結局。

- My friends and I always enjoy a Jim Carrey **comedy**.
  我朋友和我總是很喜歡金凱瑞演的**喜劇**。

conflict 戲劇衝突

故事主要的角色較量、勢力對抗或想法衝突。

- *Dr. Jekyll and Mr. Hyde* illustrates the **conflict** between good and evil.
  《變身怪醫》描述善惡之間的**衝突**。

conclusion 尾聲

解決情節衝突的方法，使故事結束。

- That play's **conclusion** was very satisfying. Every conflict was resolved. 該劇的**結局**十分令人滿意，所有的衝突都被圓滿解決。

dialogue 對白

小說或戲劇角色所說的話語。

- Amusing **dialogue** is an important element of most comedies.
  有趣的**對白**是大多喜劇中一項重要的元素。

drama 戲劇

故事，通常非喜劇類型，特別是寫來讓演員在戲劇或電影中演出。

- The TV **drama** about spies was very suspenseful.
  那齣關於間諜的電視**劇**非常懸疑。

event 事件

發生的事情；特別的事。

- The most exciting **event** in the story was the surprise ending.
  故事中最精彩的**事件**是意外的結局。

introduction 簡介

一篇簡短的文章，呈現並解釋小說或戲劇的劇情。

■ The **introduction** to *Frankenstein* is in the form of a letter.
《科學怪人》的**簡介**是以信件的型式呈現。

---

motive 動機

一股內在或外在的力量，迫使角色做出某些事情。

■ What was that character's **motive** for telling a lie?
那個角色說謊的**動機**為何？

---

passage 段落

書寫作品的部分內容，範圍短至一行，長至幾段。

■ His favorite **passage** from the book described the author's childhood.
他在書中最喜歡的**段落**描述了該作者的童年。

---

playwright 劇作家

戲劇的作者。

■ William Shakespeare is the world's most famous **playwright**.
威廉莎士比亞是世界上最知名的**劇作家**。

---

plot 情節

故事或戲劇中一連串的因果事件，導致最終結局。

■ The **plot** of that mystery story is filled with action.
該推理故事的**情節**充滿打鬥。

---

point of view 觀點

由角色的心理層面來看待故事發展的狀況。

■ The father's **point of view** about elopement was quite different from the daughter's. 父親對於私奔的**看法**與女兒迥然不同。

prologue 序幕

在戲劇第一幕開始前的介紹。

- The playwright described the main characters in the **prologue** to the play.

  劇作家在**序幕**中描述了主要角色。

quotation 名句

被引述的文句；某角色所說的詞語；在引號內的文字。

- A popular **quotation** from *Julius Caesar* begins, "Friends, Romans, countrymen . . ."

  《凱薩大帝》中**常被引用的文句**開頭是：「各位朋友，各位羅馬人，各位同胞……」。

role 角色

演員在劇中揣摩表演的人物。

- Who would you like to see play the **role** of Romeo?

  你想看誰飾演羅密歐這個**角色**呢？

sequence 順序

故事或事件發生的時序。

- Sometimes actors rehearse their scenes out of **sequence**.

  演員有時會不按**順序**排練他們出場的戲。

setting 情節背景

故事發生的地點與時間。

- This play's **setting** is New York in the 1940s.

  戲劇的**背景**設定於 1940 年代的紐約。

soliloquy 獨白

角色向觀眾發表想法的一番言論，猶如自言自語。

- One famous **soliloquy** is Hamlet's speech that begins, "To be, or not to be . . ."
  哈姆雷特最知名的**獨白**是：「生，抑或是死……」。

---

symbol 象徵

用以代表其他事物的人或物。

- In Hawthorne's famous novel, the scarlet letter is a **symbol** for adultery.
  在霍桑知名的小說中，紅字是姦淫罪的**象徵**。

---

theme 主題

戲劇或小說的主要意義；中心思想。

- Ambition and revenge are common **themes** in Shakespeare's plays.
  在莎士比亞的劇作中，雄心壯志與報復是常見的**主題**。

---

tragedy 悲劇

嚴肅且有悲傷結局的戲劇。

- *Macbeth*, the shortest of Shakespeare's plays, is a **tragedy**.
  莎士比亞最短的劇作《馬克白》是部**悲劇**。